CROSSING
THE
STREAM

CROSSING THE STREAM

ELIZABETH-IRENE BAITIE

ACCORD BOOKS

NORTON YOUNG READERS

AN IMPRINT OF W. W. NORTON & COMPANY
INDEPENDENT PUBLISHERS SINCE 1923

To my entire family, the wings that lifted me.

For information about permission to reproduce selections from this book, write to
Permissions, W. W. Norton & Company, Inc., 500 Fifth Avenue, New York, NY 10110

For information about special discounts for bulk purchases, please contact
W. W. Norton Special Sales at specialsales@wwnorton.com or 800-233-4830

Manufacturing by LSC Communications, Harrisonburg
Book design by Beth Steidle
Production manager: Beth Steidle

ISBN 978-1-324-01709-7

W. W. Norton & Company, Inc., 500 Fifth Avenue, New York, N.Y. 10110
www.wwnorton.com

W. W. Norton & Company Ltd., 15 Carlisle Street, London W1D 3BS

0 9 8 7 6 5 4 3 2 1

PROLOGUE

◇ ◇ ◇ ◇ ◇ ◇ ◇ ◇ ◇

ATO FROZE MID-STEP, HIS MOUTH DRY.

No. No. No.

He glanced around wildly. Behind him were the trees. Beside him rose the rock with purple thistle. Ahead was the pond, circled by dead water plants, reflecting the sun on its still surface. Beyond it were the vegetable rows, and past those—the House of Fire. Everything was still here. Everything except . . .

His legs could not hold him up. Stumbling forward, he sank to his knees.

He pressed his fists against the sting in his eyes. Still, a tear trickled down, along the corner of his lips, warm and salty, dripping down his chin.

It was over. They had come so close. But like everything else, the dream was dead.

And he had wanted so hard to be good enough to go.

CHAPTER ONE

◊ ◊ ◊ ◊ ◊ ◊ ◊ ◊ ◊

Several weeks earlier

ATO STARED AT THE PRINT ON THE SCHOOL BULLETIN BOARD.
His breathing stopped.

Nnoma spreads its wings in welcome to Asafo—Earth Warriors.
Are you old enough to leave home on your own, but young
enough to believe that the earth needs you?
Do you have a project to protect the green earth, the blue sky,
and the animals and people between the two?
Show us!
Then let us ferry you away from the crowded city to the
mountainous bird island of
NNOMA.

"Your project is your invitation. Submit it to us by June first,"
Ato read. That was twelve weeks from now.

Nnoma was open at last! A vision of the island flooded Ato's mind—rock-studded mountainsides and leafy lower hills. He had sailed over the choppy gray waters that surrounded the bird island a thousand times—in his dreams. He had landed on its famous eastern peak, the Dawn Locus, where the first rays of sunrise struck in an explosion of red and orange light. Here, thousands of bird species lived protected, including his favorite bird—the peregrine falcon.

"Move!"

"How long does it take you to read that?"

"We all want to have a look!"

Ato had seen all he needed to. Beside him, Dzifa elbowed out a path for them through the mass of sweaty school kids surging toward the bulletin board.

"Ato, we've got to get in!" Her small, heart-shaped face was alight with excitement.

Yes, they did, Ato thought, heart pounding, as they walked down the school corridor to join another friend, Leslie.

Leslie pointed to Ato's hands. "That's because Nnoma's open?" he asked in surprise.

Ato looked down: his hands were trembling. He clenched them into fists, and flanked by his two oldest friends, he walked toward the parking lot.

The last time Nnoma had opened was when he was seven years old. It had been five years of dreaming since then. Five years dreaming about visiting the famous bird wonderland that his father had helped to build. His father had written him one letter. Its words had played on repeat in his head since he'd learned to read:

> *My son, it's been months of hard work, but now the dream is forming before my eyes. I'm sitting at the highest point of Nnoma: it's called the Dawn Locus. One day I hope you will sit here with me.*
>
> *Ato, now that the Nnoma dream is here, it must stay alive. Those of us who believe in it must protect it. For now, the sun shines, but enemy storms are gathering. One day they may be unleashed. If they are, I have a plan. It is protected, somewhere below this rock peak where the sunlight first greets Nnoma, where the falcons watch over the valley. With enough Asafo, we can protect this dream. Whenever I hold you in my arms, I can see you are truly like me—Asafo, a protector of our world.*
>
> *When your steps are strong enough to match mine, we shall walk this mountainside together, to protect this dream. Only a few people are privileged enough to step on Nnoma. You will be one of them. You'll prove yourself good enough to come here. I've asked Mummy to blow on your little toes to make you laugh. One day, your toes will be firm enough to grip this rock.*

Ato halted in the middle of the open school corridor. "We need to start our project. Now."

Leslie stuck out his lip doubtfully. "D'you know people can get diseases and parasites from infected birds?"

"No negative vibes!" Dzifa shoved back her spectacles and gave Leslie a warning look.

Being in the same school was the only thing his two friends had in common. Good thing Dzifa had stopped biting kids the way she used to back in kindergarten, Ato thought, or she'd have eaten Leslie alive by now. Even at twelve years old she still looked as if she wanted to deal with problems kindergarten-style.

"Why is Nnoma such a big deal? Do we really want to hang out with a bunch of birds with fleas and viruses?" Leslie's shoulders sagged with a lack of enthusiasm.

Trust Leslie, Ato thought. Always figuring out how something could not be done. "Maybe because it's the biggest bird sanctuary in all of Africa, Leslie?" he said. "Maybe because nobody knows when it's going to open? And when it does open, only a few people get to visit at a time, 'cos birds need protection from humans?" And maybe, he thought, because my father needs to know he was right about me: I am good enough to go there.

Leslie was typically unconvinced. "Think, guys: There'll be dangerous hills. Birds with chicks and bad tempers. And snakes, 'cos snakes eat bird eggs. Even if we do get in, I bet something bad will happen. Remember when those Year Ten guys sneaked in spray paint on the school trip to Cape Coast and vando—vandili—"

"Vandalized," Dzifa snapped.

"Yeah, did that to the monument. The whole class got sent back and school trips were canceled the rest of the year. Imagine if a group of kids like that got to Nnoma this year? Imagine! We'd all get thrown out and Nnoma would never open again."

Leslie was so like a parakeet, Ato thought. Cheep-chirp-cheep . . . as he backed out of everything. Unlike Dzifa. She always reminded him of a magpie: flying face-first *into* everything.

"Leslie"—Dzifa swept her forefinger across her lips in a zip-up motion—"stay home. We'll send you pictures from Nnoma."

"We will?" Ato asked.

Leslie plowed on. "Ato, I know—your dad wrote something about some secret plan on Nnoma. Whatever plan he left, the rats would have gotten to it by now. Rats eat paper. And bird eggs."

Ato felt the blood rush to his head. When Leslie talked like that, it made him wish he'd never mentioned his dad's letter to him. "You don't know that, Leslie," he said, forcing his voice to stay steady. "Besides, we've been planning this project to get into Nnoma for years. And we're starting. Tomorrow."

"But we'll be up against so many other projects. We don't stand a chance!"

"Ato"—Dzifa adjusted the strap of her gym bag on her skinny shoulders—"don't listen to him. We're on. Tomorrow. And now it's basketball for me. See you later!" With a wave of her twiggy arms, she darted off toward the playing court.

Ato watched her go with a stab of envy. He was never allowed to stay behind for after-school games. His mother believed hanging about after classes made children wayward. If Dzifa went straight home after school, she wouldn't be so wild, Ato had heard Leslie's mother say. Ato's mother had agreed. They praised Leslie for being happy to go home right after class. It didn't seem to matter that he went home to play games on his phone.

Ato wove his way beside Leslie through the mass of school kids chattering like a thousand sparrows in the open corridor. His mother was waiting, as usual. So was Leslie's. Their cars were parked underneath the tree at the far end of the school parking lot. Ato darted over to her through slow-moving parking lot traffic.

"Good afternoon, Mum!" He yanked open his mother's passenger door and landed with a thump on the front seat. "Guess what?!"

"Ato, one day my car door will fall off, the way you open it."

He knew that voice. It was mainly "I'm tired," a hint of "Not enough customers bought anything from the shop," with a smidgen of "Your voice is too loud." And today there was something else . . .

"Good afternoon, dear." She cranked her grumpy engine and inched toward the gate. Home was only a twenty-minute walk away—a ten-minute run for Ato—but his mother insisted on closing up shop to take him home. Then she went back to work to worry about things, or to meetings to worry about other things.

She had to hear his news. "Mum?"

She got her news in first. "Ato, you're going to Nana's this weekend. To sleep over."

He stared at her.

She kept the car moving, hands clutching the wheel. Thin veins rose on the back of her hands, like brown worms.

"Nana's? Why?"

"Next weekend too. Every weekend, Ato."

Her jaw was clenched.

Wow. She wasn't joking.

CHAPTER TWO

◇ ◇ ◇ ◇ ◇ ◇ ◇ ◇ ◇

"IT'S FRIDAY THE THIRTEENTH TOMORROW. SOME DAY TO BE going to your creepy nana's. I'd be worried if I were you, Ato," Leslie said, pulling on thick green gardening gloves.

Ato felt a stab of annoyance. Mum and Leslie's mother talked a lot about Nana. He kept his eyes on the holes he was poking with his finger in the soil—six inches apart, two lettuce seeds per hole. "You're not me, Leslie."

Leslie's gloves weren't the only thick things around. "Why is your mum making you go? My mum says your nana—"

"Leslie." Dzifa squinted up from her position a few feet from Ato. She was dropping okra seeds into her holes. "You're not even supposed to be here. Can you stop being pointless? Or go home?"

Leslie shut up and picked up the watering can.

Ato was glad. He didn't want to know what Leslie's mum had said about Nana. It would probably upset him. Leslie was here because his mum had heard about Nnoma's opening on the news; she'd made him join their project at once. Ato had overheard her tell his mum that Nnoma was looking for kids exactly like her

9

Leslie—clever and responsible. Having Leslie join them wasn't so bad, Ato reasoned: he had a phone—it would be useful for taking pictures of their project.

Ato couldn't count the number of times he and Dzifa had talked about this Nnoma project: growing vegetables using only organic natural pesticides. They'd made a pesticide with natural black soap that had been good at keeping bugs away. All they'd been waiting for was the announcement about Nnoma opening. They'd always known the project would be right here, at Turo. Turo was their patch, the wild green stretch in their neighborhood that they'd claimed as their own. It was a five-minute walk from home, three minutes if Ato was running. And if he were a diving falcon, it would be a few blurry seconds. Turo had space, too. It was twenty long paces down and across, several times the size of his tiny garden at home.

Turo was their getaway. For years, he and Dzifa and Leslie had come here to play pilolo, grumble about teachers and eat green mangoes till they had the runs. The rock at Turo was rectangular, like a wide cabinet. It was their safe perch from parents and chores. From that stone throne, they argued about which one of them would be richest in future, while tossing pebbles into the pond, watching them plop and vanish into its murky depths. He and Dzifa would wade into the water to watch bubbles rising to the surface, and to tear up pondweed and reeds to weave into little mats.

And there were evenings when he came here alone and sat on Turo's rock. In his mind, he was a peregrine falcon, and the rock was the peak of the Dawn Locus. He would watch the sky turn orange and purple at sunset and dream that it was sunrise at Nnoma. And he could hear his dad telling him: I knew you'd make it, son. I knew you'd make me proud. At those times, the only sounds around Turo were tweeting birds in the crescent of palm trees behind them and lizards scuttling in the undergrowth. Occasionally Papa Kojo's grunts would carry over the pond as he and his sons worked their vegetable lots.

It was from years of watching Papa Kojo using bags of chemical sprays to protect his plants from bugs that Ato and Dzifa had dreamt of their Nnoma project. The plan was to show their vegetables to the locals, and convince Papa Kojo to switch to organic pesticides.

The day before, they'd cleared weeds from their spot. The plan was simple. Ato and Dzifa would plant the vegetable seeds— lettuce, radish, okra, spring onions, corn and spinach. Leslie would water them.

Lettuce seeds planted, Ato started on the radish, two seeds per hole again, and began to think about the coming weekend. So Mum was finally letting him go to Nana's. He had memories of happy trips to Nana's when he was much younger. But suddenly, those visits had stopped. He remembered the last one—Nana's birthday party. He'd only been seven years old then; he remembered dancing madly to music, eating too much and falling asleep on her porch sofa. They'd never been back since. Nana had asked to have him several times, but Mum always had a different reason why he couldn't go. After a while, Nana stopped asking. She visited them, though, regular as sunrise—every first Sunday, every birthday, and at Christmas, and she would talk to him about things he liked—like falcons and hunting birds. On these visits, Mum would sit in the armchair right across from Nana, watching a lot, saying very little.

Nana would ask Mum how she was.

"Everything's fine, thank you, Nana," Mum would always say with that tight little smile.

It wasn't true, Ato knew. Everything wasn't fine. He'd overheard Mum on the phone when she had her weekly call with the Prophet, telling him how hard it was to pay bills and to bring up a son alone. Mum always seemed to feel better after her phone calls with the Prophet. That made Ato glad . . . partly. There was one thing that confused him: the Prophet kept telling Mum to be careful of Nana. He couldn't ask Mum about that, though, because he wasn't supposed to be listening in on her conversation. He was supposed to be doing his homework in his room. It wasn't like he had his ear to the wall or anything. But her phone was on speaker, in the living room—right next to his bedroom, and he couldn't help but hear every word.

Ato looked up. Leslie was trudging back with the watering can from a standpipe several yards away.

"Hey, Leslie! You're using tap water? What's wrong with this?" Ato pointed ahead where, a few feet away, Turo sloped softly to meet the water's edge.

"Germy pond," Leslie panted. "I'm not dying of typhoid or chorela because of some birds on an island."

"Cholera," Dzifa corrected.

"Whatever, Dzifa. I'm not like you, eating street food and messing around with germs."

"I eat street food, yeah. But I've never had cholera."

Ato's taste buds zinged. Dzifa's mother bought street waakye wrapped in shiny green leaves. Once, he'd had a meal with them on a rickety bench at the street-side waakye stall. Afterward, they'd washed their hands over the gutter. It'd been the best waakye he'd ever had. His mum's home-cooked waakye didn't compare to it, and he'd been dumb enough to tell her so. That week, on speakerphone with the Prophet of Fire, his mother had complained about how hard life was for her, doing everything alone for over ten years. How much easier it was for Dzifa's mum to buy street food instead of cooking at home. How street waakye sellers didn't pick out the old holey beans; they just tossed them into the pot along with weevils and moldy rice and food additives that gave you cancer. The Prophet of Fire had agreed, and told her softly that children often had a Spirit of Ingratitude. Ato never mentioned street waakye again.

Leslie was sprinkling tap water over their newly planted seeds. He'd always had a phobia about germs, Ato thought in resignation. Even when they were younger, it was usually just him and Dzifa who got muddy in the water.

Leslie slipped off his gloves, removed his phone from his pocket and tapped at the screen. He flashed it at them. "Look what it says here about what you get from dirty water: dysentery and hepatititi—"

"Hepatitis." Dzifa's voice was curt.

"Uh, huh. And all that. Did you know that hundreds of thousands of people die from these diseases every year?"

"Sissy," she teased. "You've got no immunity. If the pond is good enough for Papa Kojo's vegetables, it should be good enough for ours!"

"You can trek to the tap till next year, Leslie," Ato said. "So long as we get this job done." Water was water anyway, he thought, wherever it came from. And Leslie was just the sort of kid who would actually catch some rare bug from the pond and get sick. If that happened, Leslie's mother would never let them hear the end of it.

Dzifa returned to stabbing holes in the ground for spinach seeds. For a while the only sounds were their breathing and the rising chanting from the House of Fire: it meant a meeting was ending. Ato concentrated on spacing out the spinach seeds. He avoided the spot by the rock where prickly purple thistle grew. Its spikes stuck to clothes and had to be pinched out with tweezers, much to his mum's annoyance.

Why was he going to Nana's tomorrow? The thought circled around in his brain. "I'm scared," he'd heard his mother whisper to the Prophet of Fire. And he'd heard the Prophet gently warn her over and over again: "History repeats itself. Be Very Careful about Nana's sofa. And her strange potions. And Nana's spirit: Grandmothers have Powerful Spirits."

What history was the Prophet talking about? What was up with Nana's sofa? Was that the same one he'd fallen asleep on all those years ago? In the past he'd asked Mum why he couldn't go to Nana's. She had clamped her lips together and told him to be content with his own home. He couldn't understand. If he had to be so careful about Nana and her sofa and her potions and her powerful spirit, then why was Mum making him go?

Ato glanced at Dzifa's patch and picked up speed. She'd planted twice as many seeds as he had. The tall grass nearby parted, and a brown blur streaked out and leapt at him. Ato toppled backward on the grassy earth.

"Choco!"

Ato grabbed the dog's neck and play-wrestled her to the ground. She wriggled out of his grip and sniffed Leslie's feet, who patted her head gingerly with his re-gloved hands. With a yip, the dog bounded onto Dzifa's chest, all pink tongue and stubby wagging tail. Dzifa sat on the ground, allowing Choco to raise her front paws onto her shoulders and lick her face too.

Ato reached into his pocket. "Here, Choco!"

The dog snapped the chicken drumstick Ato held out and scampered to a ledge beneath the rock, where she crouched down and began gnawing at it. No one knew who Choco belonged to. She was as much a part of Turo as the pond, the trees and Papa Kojo's vegetable patches.

Papa Kojo approached the bank of the pond opposite and waved at them, his spaced-out teeth glinting in the sun. "I donno why dis dog dusn' follo you to school," he chuckled, nudging his hose deeper into the pond. Papa Kojo whistled to Choco. She gulped down the remains of her bone and pranced on small paws toward him, stopping by the pond to lap the water.

Ato liked Papa Kojo. Everyone in their community bought his fresh vegetables. Years ago, when he was little, Papa Kojo would hoist him onto his hefty shoulders while his mother picked out her veggies. Back then, he would "help" Papa Kojo haul up his tin watering cans from the pond. Most of the water would have spilled out by the time he had struggled to the vegetable beds, but Papa Kojo would still high-five him and call him "champion boy." Even now, he always gave Mum an extra cabbage when she bought his vegetables. "For champion boy," he would say.

Papa Kojo's hose connected to a watermelon-sized pump that hummed as it drew water up to be sprayed over the vegetable beds. "Champion boy, you kids wan' become farmers too?"

Ato explained their project to Papa Kojo, who listened closely.

"It's okay for you," he shrugged when Ato had finished. "You're kids playin'. But if you haf to pay rent an' feed moufs, you gotta go for de powerful stuff—de chemicals." He scratched his thick neck, and turned to look at his vegetable plots. A crease of concern formed on his brow. "This season sumtin' is not right, de cabbage—"

But his words were cut short. A roar rose from beyond his vegetable lots:

"FIRE!"

"FIRE!"

"FIRE!"

CHAPTER THREE

◊ ◊ ◊ ◊ ◊ ◊ ◊ ◊ ◊

FOR YEARS THE SMALL BUILDING WITH NO ROOF THAT STOOD a few yards up from Papa Kojo's vegetable plots had been empty. A dusty patch of earth stretched out in front of the building. Yellow-and-white taxis lined up there to carry folk into town. Women sat in the building's shade, behind wooden tables where they dozed in between selling bananas, roasted groundnuts and flimsy plastic toys.

Everyone noticed when a slender man wearing smart clothes and gold-rimmed glasses appeared. A few people met with him in the building on weekends to sing and clap. The unfinished building got a roof. The waiting taxis moved away. Pretty soon the building had windows and a shiny wooden front door. More folk gathered on weekends and some weekdays to sing and clap. The sleepy sellers packed up their crude wood tables and moved away. The building got a smooth coat of yellow paint and a billboard rose in front of it. It bore the slender man's picture, with an orange flame of fire shooting from the tip of his forefinger. In thick letters, the billboard announced:

YAKAYAKA—PROPHET OF FIRE
Fiery Gatherings: Sunday 9 a.m.
Fiery Miracles: Monday 5 p.m.
Fiery Prophecies: Tuesday 5 p.m.
Fiery Revelations: Thursday 5 p.m.
Fiery Deliverances: Friday 5 p.m.
Free weekly counseling phone calls

Electric lights lit up the building, inside and outside. More people flocked over to sing and clap and shout "Fire!" Ato could hear them from his home, thanks to the loudspeakers fixed to the wall outside the building. Bush and weeds around the building were cleared, and smooth red earth was laid down to make space for cars. On some days benches and blue canopies had to be set outside to seat extra people.

When the Prophet shouted "Fire," amazing things happened; Ato had heard this from his mum and Leslie and Philomena, the local cleaning lady.

On Miracle Monday, when the Prophet shouted "Fire," he could burn away a person's problems—problems like not having a job, or not having any friends, or being sick for a long time.

On Prophecy Tuesday, when the Prophet shouted "Fire," he could tell people what would happen to them in future—if they were going to have a dreadful car accident or win a lot of money.

On Revelation Thursday, when the Prophet shouted "Fire," he could tell people why odd things were happening to them—why the fruit tree in their garden had suddenly withered, or why they kept having bad luck.

And Deliverance Friday—that was a big day. That was when the Prophet shouted "Fire" to drive out mean spirits that lived inside people. The spirits were powerful and made bad things happen to the people they lived in. They would fight hard to stay inside the people, but the Prophet was more powerful. Ato had heard that people shook violently and fainted when they were being delivered from spirits on Deliverance Friday.

Out in the community, the Prophet gave out scarves to the women and handkerchiefs to the men and sweets to the children. The Prophet had a refuge in the countryside where he looked after kids who had no homes. It was very kind of the Prophet to look after those lonely children, Ato thought. Lucky for him, he had Mum. Otherwise he might have been like those kids with no mum and dad.

Ato's mum went to the House of Fire two or three evenings a week. He knew she wished she could go more often, but she had to look after her shop; she couldn't afford an extra hand. Leslie's mum went to every meeting. Dzifa's mum had called the police on the Prophet and complained that the loudspeakers disturbed her mental tranquility. She was an interior decorator. She couldn't plan designs peacefully with that racket going on, she told the police. After that, the loudspeakers at the House of Fire were turned down as the sun went down. Ato had heard his mother and Leslie's mother talk about Dzifa's mother. They didn't say kind things, so he didn't tell Dzifa.

From where he knelt in Turo, Ato could see his mum stepping out of the House of Fire in her gray dress. She spoke to Prophet Yakayaka, who was standing on the front steps chatting with the people streaming out. Ato knew his mother had problems she wanted the Prophet to burn away, like not having enough money. She also wanted to burn up anything that stopped Ato from being like his father: Not Writing His Homework Tidily and Keeping His Closet Messy. She always told him how Responsible and Sensible his father had been. It made him feel bad that he wasn't more like his father.

Soon everyone had left the House of Fire. Prophet Yakayaka was walking in their direction now. Philomena bobbed along beside him carrying his briefcase, with her braids bunched on her head like a pineapple.

As the Prophet approached them, Leslie tugged off his gloves. He took out a packet of sanitary hand wipes from his backpack.

"In case he wants to shake hands with us," he urged, handing the packet to Ato and Dzifa.

The Prophet had arrived at the point where the lane split into two paths—one leading to Papa Kojo's lots, the other winding around Turo and toward the town. Papa Kojo and his sons and workers waved at Prophet Yakayaka, grinning. The Prophet waved back and shouted something about good work. Philomena waved at them too.

Dzifa's sharp nose twitched in amusement. "Philomena thinks carrying his stuff makes her an assistant prophet."

Ato observed Philomena's plump, blotchy face. She did look very proud to be helping the Prophet. Then again, who wouldn't be? Philomena got by cleaning and cooking in neighborhood homes. She lived for free in the shed in Ato's garden. In exchange, she cleaned house for them. The shed opened to a lane outside, so she could come in and go out without having to use the front door of the house. She cleaned the House of Fire too—and made sure everyone heard about that.

Philomena would have been okay to have around if she wasn't so nosy. Last week she had fished out his collection of dead insects from his closet and showed them to Mum. Mum had shrieked in horror and told the Prophet about it on her next phone chat with him. Ato was Obsessed with Death, the Prophet had said in a soft, firm voice. He had ordered the insects to be burned. Ato didn't understand the fuss over dead insects that couldn't bite anyone. It had taken months to collect them, too. Philomena had no business in his closet. She'd probably gone to peek into the bottom drawer where Mum kept clothes she didn't want and was going to give away. He suspected Philomena rifled through to see what she could help herself to.

Philomena probably also had a lot of stuff she wanted the Prophet to burn—she was afraid of everything. She scolded Ato for whistling at night, saying it called up ghosts from their graves. When he left his fingernail clippings on the floor, she told him evil spirits would now have bits of him to carry out devilish acts on. She warned him not to fall asleep in strange places: people would breathe their spirits into him and take over his body. Just yesterday, a little bird had begun building a nest in the eaves at home. That bird could be a magic spy, she'd warned him darkly.

Philomena had told Leslie that people might sprinkle a powder into his drink before he put his glass to his lips: once he drank from it, he would be their zombie forever. Leslie believed her. He had no desire to drink out of cups or glasses away from home anyway, just in case they hadn't been washed properly and had other people's germs clinging to the rim, waiting to infect him.

Dzifa had once picked up a coin on the road. Philomena had been aghast. She'd told Dzifa a story about a girl who'd picked up a fifty-cedi note outside her front door: the next morning the girl had been found in bed—transformed into a tuber of yam. The bewitched note had been left there by her enemy. Dzifa had laughed in her face and asked how a grown-up woman could believe such silly Ananse stories. She'd called Philomena ignorant. Ato's mother had overheard, and asked Dzifa to apologize. Dzifa had refused. Mum had not been pleased. Dzifa was a wild child, Ato heard her telling the Prophet later that night.

The Prophet turned right onto the track toward them. He dabbed his high, glistening forehead with a spotless white handker-chief. His straight teeth gleamed white through his tidy black mustache and beard.

"Children," he cooed, soft as a pigeon. He flicked an invisible speck of dust from his jacket sleeve.

Ato straightened up quickly and brushed his hands. He didn't want to look like a dirty ruffian to this man. Leslie was already standing stiff as a brush with his hands respectfully behind him. Dzifa remained on her knees, still counting seeds under her breath.

"No homework? No chores to help your parents? Nothing to do apart from getting into mischief in the mud?"

Philomena pursed her lips as if they'd been caught eating mud pies.

"Umm . . ." Ato started, feeling confused. Was planting seeds a mischievous thing to do?

"Erm . . ." Leslie began.

"It's not mischief. It's a project," Dzifa said from the ground.

"You must use time meaningfully. Help your parents. Study hard in school—"

"This is a meaningful project. For a very meaningful place," Dzifa continued.

"Stop interrupting."

"But you're not listening." Her tone was sharp.

There was silence. Ato gulped. Leslie looked ready to faint. Philomena threw Dzifa a you-again look.

Prophet Yakayaka wagged a finger at Dzifa. "The Spirit of Disrespect."

Dzifa's eyes flashed like black pebbles. Ato's heart lurched. She was in magpie mode—bristling to attack.

"I don't have a Spirit of Disrespect. I have a Spirit of me."

To Ato's relief, Prophet Yakayaka was already walking off and did not see Dzifa's deepening scowl. Philomena glanced back at them. Shame on you, her eyes said.

Ato felt himself go hot all over. "You shouldn't speak like that to him, Dzifa; he's the Prophet of Fire!"

"I don't care! He should've kept his spirits to himself."

Ato returned to his seeds, feeling troubled. Sometimes he wished Dzifa would hold back a little; the Prophet was a powerful person.

CHAPTER FOUR

◊ ◊ ◊ ◊ ◊ ◊ ◊ ◊ ◊

THE NEXT DAY, AFTER SCHOOL, ATO SAT STRAPPED INTO THE passenger seat of his mother's car as they drove over to Nana's. Tat-tat-tat. Her red nails rapped at the tattered gray cover of her steering wheel. They looked like dancing blood droplets. Crimson nail polish was the only bright color she ever wore. All her clothes were brown and gray or black.

Mum was unhappy with him. Her small lips were turned down at the corners, and her eyes blinked her concern.

"Ato, a turkey killing a dog? Why did you draw that during Art? Why didn't you draw sunflowers like you were supposed to?" She wove past a slow taxi with a "tut" and gave the driver a side-eye.

Ato kept his mouth shut. It didn't matter what he said, Mum was still going to be upset. It wasn't even a turkey, but that's what Leslie's mother had said it was. He wiped away upper lip sweat with the back of his hand. Mum's car air conditioner had conked out months ago—like her back door handles and the seat recliner. She only fixed broken stuff if the car couldn't move without them. So he'd gotten used to sweating in the car and to new rattling noises.

His mother jerked a thumb toward the backseat, where his drawing lay. "When children draw pictures like that, it's a sign of something wrong. Your father would have been so disappointed to see such a violent drawing from you."

Ato leaned around and nudged the rolled-up drawing into his weekend bag. His father would have known that out in the wild, it was a dog-eat-dog world, he thought. Inside he felt heavy, like a lump of clay. Would he ever measure up to his dad? Sometimes he wondered—was he as good as his father had thought he was?

"Ato, if anyone saw that drawing, they'd think I was a bad parent."

He knew who "anyone" was—Prophet Yakayaka.

"I'd like you to be more like your father, to behave yourself, not act like a wild child. He was a special person; that's how he got chosen to help build Nnoma. And I know you want to go there, but there'll be lots of very intelligent children trying to get in. It's going to be a long shot, so don't get your hopes up."

Ato didn't want to be trapped in the car listening to this. He was a peregrine falcon with stiff, pointed wings that could lift him off the ground better than a jet plane could. He could fly out of the car, up into the sky, nearly a mile high. He would fly all the way to his target, Nnoma, and settle down on the Dawn Locus. Then he would read his father's letter aloud.

One day I hope you will sit here with me, Ato . . . Whenever I hold you in my arms, I can see you are truly like me . . . You'll prove yourself good enough to come here.

And up there at the peak of the Dawn Locus, close to heaven, his father would hear him and know he'd been right about his son.

His mother honked at a street hawker, jolting him out of his daydream. They were in the traffic that snaked down Liberation Road like a giant centipede. Men and women dawdled alongside the moving centipede, balancing trays on their heads. They sold velvet tamarind and frozen yogurt and tangerines and groundnuts boiled in their shells. He longed for a bag of velvet tamarind, but he knew better than to ask his mother to buy anything from hawkers who hadn't washed their hands.

After about half an hour, they turned onto a wide, quiet street. There were no street hawkers here. TAMARIND RIDGE VILLE, a large sign at the corner of the road announced. This was Nana's side of town. Ato stared. Wavy palm trees on either side of the road bowed to homes with sweeping balconies that made them look like castles. Electrical wiring stretched along the tops of most walls. Electrical wiring meant rich people with expensive stuff they wanted to protect from thieves. Left turn. Right. Another left turn. The houses were painted in soft blues and pinks and peaches, unlike in his community where every home was a dull white or fading yellow color.

Tat-tat-tat. Mum's fingertips fluttered again on her wheel like nervous rose petals. She slowed to a stop alongside a butter-yellow wall with a riot of peach, white and purple bougainvillea blossoms twisting along the top of it. He peeked through the diamond-shaped gaps in the stone wall. It was just as he remembered—a huge leafy garden. Nana's house sat in the middle like a sweet candy home on a green carpet surrounded by a magic wood. Back home, four big hops would take him from their front door to their wooden gate. They didn't have a lawn; Mum couldn't afford a gardener.

His mother turned to him with her engine still running.

"Ato"—her tone had shifted from cross to nervous—"listen to me: Don't sit on her porch sofa. Please. And don't tell her I told you that."

He stared at her.

"Promise me," she urged.

Be careful of that porch sofa, the Prophet had said. History repeats itself.

"I . . ." he began, but the small blue side gate was already swinging open. Nana swirled out like a joyful yellow and green bird of paradise. She must have been waiting. Her skirt reminded him of old and new mango leaves.

"Ato!" She hopped across the narrow concrete pavement and opened his car door. Her arms enveloped him when he stepped out. She was smiling, kissing his cheeks and forehead. His head had inched past her ear now, he realized. The familiar smell of shea butter and talcum powder wafted delicately to him. It was a smell he loved.

I'm scared. Why had his mother said that so often to the Prophet? And why did the Prophet keep telling Mum to be careful?

His mother switched off her engine and stepped out of the car.

She brushed a twitching hand down her skirt and began to tell Nana about his homework and class tests and bedtime. But Nana had already slung his weekend bag over her square shoulder and was pulling him toward her gate.

"Mina." The smile faded from Nana's face. There was something in her voice—almost sadness. "Let's stick with our plan."

And she whisked Ato through the gate. It clanged shut like a jail door. His mother was left outside, by the open door of her car.

Ato had heard the plan: Mum would bring him to Nana's on Friday after school. On Sunday after lunch, Nana would take him back home. He could do his homework at home: Nana's time with him was not for homework.

Nana skipped ahead, up the stairs to the wide rectangular front porch of her home. He hung back, beside the gate.

"Nana, Mum is still outside."

"She won't be there forever," Nana called back lightly. "Stretch your legs in the garden and then come see your room." She disappeared behind the screen door, taking his bag inside.

He looked up at the porch. A lush green creeper dotted with cup-shaped lavender flowers wound through a wooden lattice that framed the space. Red clay pots squatted along the porch walls, each sprouting plants with zigzag-edged leaves, furry red leaves and pointed needle leaves. And there it was. At the far end of the porch. The sofa.

It was a lumpy three-seater covered in scratchy-looking orange fabric. It had been patched in a few places and was stained in several more. It looked like it had been rescued from a sofa orphanage. What happened after a person sat on it? Did Mum and the Prophet think it was bewitched? Two cane chairs with green cushions were set opposite it, across a porch table. Hopefully it would be safe to sit on them.

His mother hadn't moved. He would have heard her clattery engine above the evening conversations of people walking back from work on the street outside. Why had she brought him here if she was too scared to leave him? He fleetingly considered going back out to her.

Your father would have been so disappointed . . .

He changed his mind and turned to Nana's garden, which sprawled out to the right of the porch. Red hibiscuses grew along the creamy wall. Their long orange stalks, dusted with yellow pollen, hung out from the heart of the frilly petals. Vegetables grew along the side of the house, near the back wall. He recognized tomatoes, okra, peppers and lettuce. But the real magic rose ahead of him: he counted—one, two, three, four, five, six spreading trees. They grew way above the roof of the house.

The trees silently beckoned him. He stepped along the paving stones that wound an S-shaped path to the garden. The leafy branches allowed the setting sun to speckle the ground with bronze light. He walked past, rubbing his palm on their rough trunks—a mango tree, an avocado.

And then he saw it. Another couple of steps and he would have trod on it—a green tarpaulin rectangle spread out on the ground underneath a neem tree. A pyramid of loose earth rose beside it. He leaned forward, lifted the edge of the tarpaulin . . . and felt his heart stop. A hole in the ground—deep and rectangular. Freshly dug.

It looked like a grave.

CHAPTER FIVE

◊ ◊ ◊ ◊ ◊ ◊ ◊ ◊ ◊

ATO DROPPED THE CORNER OF THE TARPAULIN AND TOOK A step back. Why did Nana have a grave in her garden? One wrong move and he'd have been neck deep in there. Why hadn't she warned him about it?

Be careful.

I'm scared.

Overheard conversations skittered about like geckos in his head.

Calm down, he told himself. But his skin tingled all over. Until now, the sofa was all he'd had to think about. Now there was this.

Outside, his mother's Nissan engine finally coughed to life. She'd been there all this time! He could run to the comfort of her clanking car, away from this grave, to the safety of their four-hop garden. But her tires were already crunching down the dirt road. She was leaving him here, even though she didn't want to. Leaving him in an enchanted wood with an empty grave. Unwelcome fairy tales crept into his head: Hansel and Gretel abandoned by their parents in the forest. The witch's house of sweets. Rapunzel and the witch's vegetable garden. The red sun dipped lower on the horizon, snatching away warmth from the air. He shivered.

On the porch behind him, the screen door swung open. He spun around.

Nana stood with two glasses raised high. "Ato!" she called.

He approached her slowly. Philomena's tales about magic potions that would make him a zombie forever stole into his brain. They were Ananse stories, he told himself firmly.

"Pre-dinner garden fruit cocktail with my secret spices," she announced. Each glass foamed with a yellow liquid. "Make you sleep like the dead. Go wash your hands in the kitchen. Straight through the door. I'll be waiting here."

Sleep like the dead? He stepped up the porch through the door and into her living room. It was a simple room, with a whiff of furniture polish and flowery potpourri in the air. Four leather armchairs made a perfect rectangle around a glass-topped center table. The polished wood floor, like the glass top, reflected the last rays of sunlight outside. The kitchen was white and bright with a regular stove and an oven he couldn't fit into. Why did she want him to sleep like the dead? So she could breathe her spirit into him? He felt a jab of shame for allowing Philomena's Ananse stories to creep into his head and make him think this way about Nana.

Back outside on the porch with clean hands, he took his drink from Nana. She was still standing.

Strange potions. I'm scared. Zombie powder.

He sniffed it. Fruity. Perfect for disguising the smell of magic powders.

He set his drink on the porch table without tasting it.

"Why is there a hole down there, Nana?"

Her eyes flicked from him to the direction of the grave. "Don't worry about it, dear. Graves are for the dead, not the living."

So it was a grave. His heart thumped like a dancer's feet on bare earth.

"Who's dead, Nana?"

But she didn't answer. Instead she lowered herself onto the ragged orange sofa and held up a large square of paper: his drawing from school.

"This fell out of your bag." She patted the space beside her. "Sit, dear, and tell me: Did this dog know he was facing one of the most dangerous birds in the world?"

Nana could tell the bird in his drawing wasn't a turkey! Ato grinned. That was what was so cool about his grandmother. She just understood stuff that ordinary people didn't!

Nana sipped her drink. In the dimming light, shadows played about her face. Eager to find out more, he took a step toward her. Then he remembered.

Listen to me: Don't sit on her porch sofa.

He sat in the cane seat opposite her. "So you recognize that bird, Nana?"

Nana held the sheet firmly against a gust of breeze tugging at it. She pointed. "That small blue head, that horny-looking crest—

that claw—it might be a slight exaggeration of the true length, but there's no mistaking the cassowary."

Wow. "Nana, everyone else thought it was a turkey."

"Now tell me how this cassowary snuffed out its enemy." She took another sip of her drink and tossed back the trailing ends of the blue scarf she'd tied like a wide ribbon around her head.

He drew up his legs and settled cross-legged on his cushion. "So this wild dog charges up to the bird, thinking—dinner with a blueberry on top. It jumps at her."

Nana's dangly earrings swung as she shook her head. "Mistake number one. A cassowary jumps too. High. And that jump is dangerous. A downward kick can break a man's bones."

Ato stared. Not only did Nana recognize the cassowary, she knew about its deadliest move. His suspicion evaporated. He took a generous swallow of his smoothie and licked his upper lip.

"Nana, you're right! That toe claw is this long." He spread the thumb and forefinger of his left hand as far apart as he could. "The first kick got the dog there." He slid his hand across his throat.

"Slicing the jugular. Hence the fountain of blood."

"Exactly, Nana! That's why the dog's tongue is purple. All its blood has drained away here." Ato pointed unnecessarily to the pool of red around the wretched dog. He made another chopping move from his throat down to his stomach.

"Second strike. That's when the dog's insides spilled out like that?" Nana waved toward the pink sausagey area of his drawing.

Ato nodded, his respect for Nana deepening. She wasn't

freaked out by blood. She knew what happened in the wild—animals killed or were killed. Like the peregrine falcon that sometimes ate its prey while they were still alive. He took several gulps of his drink, chewing the sweet pulpy bits while they admired his drawing together. The tall bird stood balanced on one leg, fixing an evil yellow eye on Nana and Ato. Its other leg was raised, pointing forward like a goose-stepping soldier. A dagger-like claw protruded from this leg. From the tip of this claw, one crimson drop of blood hung above the miserable dog, stretched on the ground. Its open eyes managed to look dead and surprised at the same time.

"It didn't expect this, Nana; a goofy-looking blue bird with no wings to have a hidden weapon."

Nana gave him a thumbs-up. "You've got to give credit to the cassowary. Over three dozen fangs coming at her. She might have been afraid, but she stood her ground and found her mark. Respect to the artist, too—mixing red and brown paint to get the perfect shade of blood-red is a tricky job."

Ato's chest swelled. Unlike everyone else, Nana understood what his drawing was really about: a bird that had fought bravely to stay alive.

"And Nana, you know cassowaries don't chirp?"

"Fact, my dear. If you hear a deep rumble, a boom in the forest, stay safe. A cassowary's about." She drained the dregs of her smoothie and stood up. "Here, let me take that, and I'll bring out dinner."

Ato stared in surprise at his empty glass and slowly handed it over to her.

Alone across from the empty sofa, he felt a stir of unease. He had just finished a whole glass of whatever potion it was Nana had made. He didn't feel any zombification going on inside him, though.

The door swung open again and Nana emerged with a tray. Even without seeing them, he could smell the kebabs. It was dark now and she flicked on a switch behind her. The overhead porch light bathed them in a soft yellow glow.

Seeing his expression of delight, she laughed. "From a friend with a street food stand. The green salad and fried plantain are from the garden."

He fell on the spicy skewers of hot beef strips, realizing just how hungry he was. The coating of spicy suya powder crumbled onto his fingers as he stuffed his mouth.

Nana chewed her kebab slowly and thoughtfully, with her mouth closed.

"This is where your father was born, Ato." She patted the space on the sofa where she had invited him to sit earlier. "Here."

That was news. He paused chewing his kebab and stared at the cushion beside her. Why would Mum warn him against the sofa if that was where his dad had been born? He itched to ask Nana if she knew why Mum felt that way about her sofa, but he knew Mum would be cross if he did, so he bit his tongue.

"It was a rainy night in June," Nana continued softly as if she were talking to herself. "The city was flooded. There'd been a blackout. All phone lines were down. I was relaxed; I thought my baby would arrive a couple of weeks later. But suddenly that night, he was coming and I was alone on this sofa—waiting to greet him." Her voice dropped to a whisper. "I wrapped him in my print cloth and huddled here with him, watching his tiny chest rise and fall against me, with his wrinkly finger curled around mine." She gave a long sigh.

That was odd for her. Mum gave sad sighs. Not Nana.

"It started here, and . . ." She fell silent.

The sadness in her voice curled around his heart. She was holding something back. What was it?

"And what, Nana?"

Her eyes looked through and past him, as if her thoughts were traveling down an old road from long ago. Whatever it was, she did not want to say.

Ato turned back to his meal. All he knew about his dad was what Mum had told him—he'd been Good and Responsible and Kind and Sensible. He would have loved to have known his dad, he thought, filling his mouth with sweet fried plantain. Would he have been like the dads who fist-bumped their kids when they got an A in Math and high-fived them when they scored a soccer goal? Would he have shot hoops with him on Saturday and taken him to watch superheroes at the movie theater? Would his dad have freaked out if he'd seen him read books with "witch" or "wizard" or "blood" in the title—like Mum and Leslie's mother did? Would he have panicked about broken bones when he climbed a tree? The dads he knew didn't say "walk." They said "run faster."

He wished he had a memory of his dad, instead of just the letter. Sometimes he traced a finger over the words in his dad's letter to him. It made him feel as if he were touching his dad. Maybe it wasn't so bad that he didn't have any memories. Maybe Nana had so much to remember about his dad that it made her sad, and that was why she couldn't finish her kebab. He set down his fourth stick, picked clean, and rubbed his satisfied belly.

Something fluttered across Nana's eyes—a shadow of the past. A blink later and it was gone.

"Let's clear up and take you to your room. It's getting late."

A short hallway from the living room led them to a door on the right. Zebra-striped alphabet stickers stuck on the dark wooden door welcomed him.

ATO
BRAVE SMART SWIFT LOYAL

He turned to her in delight. Nana smiled and pushed the door. It opened into a room twice as big as his at home. A thrill surged through him. Against the wall was a huge bed with four fluffy pillows covered in a feather-design spread. At the foot of his bed was a rug with the same pattern. And then he looked up and gasped. A pair of eyes stared down unblinkingly. A peregrine falcon, painted on the white plasterboard, covered half the ceiling space. Its majestic wings were spread out in flight, exposing the barred pattern on its chest.

"Wooooow!" he breathed. He looked around his room. His

heart thudded with joy. It was perfect. On the wall opposite his bed, a blue bookshelf was packed from end to end with books: *Hunting Birds, Predators and Prey, How to Live Underground and Other Survival Techniques, Dogah the Crime Detective* . . . and a stack of comics. They were a world away from the books his mother bought him, stories warning about what happened to children who made the wrong friends and did the wrong things. Beside the bookshelf was a white closet. Its door swung open soundlessly. Nana already had spare sets of T-shirts and shorts folded on the shelves.

She pointed to a white door to the left of his room. "That's your bathroom, dear. Let me leave you to wash and let the night do its work. Sleep well: tomorrow we'll take a walk to the Forbidden Stream."

The Forbidden Stream? He scanned her face for an explanation but her smile gave nothing away. With a warm hug and a good-night kiss, she clicked the door shut after her and he was alone. He washed slowly and slipped beneath his sheet. His eyes stayed open. The bedside light stayed on.

Let the night do its work?

He remembered the glint in her eye when she saw his drawing, how she had admired the blood. Was that normal for a grandmother?

Let the night do its work.

He let out a long breath. The falcon stared down at him.

"Is this why you keep your eyes open?" he whispered to it.

CHAPTER SIX

◊ ◊ ◊ ◊ ◊ ◊ ◊ ◊ ◊

ATO BLINKED. HOW LONG HAD HE BEEN ASLEEP? HIS BEDSIDE lamp was a useless glint against the sunlight streaming through the crack in the blue curtains. In his dream he'd been perched on the edge of a freshly dug grave. Alongside him had sat a dog, and a cassowary. They had spent the whole night ghoulishly watching to see who would tumble in first. In spite of that, he had slept deeply. But had the night done its work?

He hurried to the bathroom. The rectangular mirror over the sink reflected his image. He smiled, feeling silly. His eyes hadn't turned black and liquid. His skin wasn't zombified. He sniffed. A familiar, enticing aroma wafted under the door.

In five minutes he had washed, changed and was following his nose. Nana's back was to him, but she turned around as soon as he entered the living room. Her morning greeting was delivered with a hug and a kiss. In a minute she was settling him at the dining table, which was draped with a purple cotton cloth and set with two place mats. No plates, no cutlery, he noticed. There

41

was a tray, though, covered with a purple napkin that bulged with promise. She whipped the napkin off.

"Nana!"

"Hot off the street, my dear. A friend brought it while you were still asleep. Now go wash your hands—we're eating this waakye straight from the leaf—the way it's meant to be eaten. I'll get some water in case your tongue bursts into flame."

She was back in a moment with a pitcher of water and two glasses. Ato struggled to keep calm watching her unwrap the shiny green leaves. Strong, smart hands, he thought, the color of deep honey. Hands that looked like they could handle anything. Nana spread the leaves to reveal the steaming mix of rice and black-eyed peas. She'd gone all out—his favorite extras were all here: powdery gari with spaghetti, fried plantain, and nestled on top of those, boiled eggs and cubes of fried beef. The leaves glistened with oil, tinged orange with spices.

His words tumbled out as the waakye went down. He told her about Nnoma opening and their project with the black soap pesticide. How badly he wanted to go. How Leslie joined only because his mother made him. How the Prophet thought they were just messing about in dirt. How his mother told the Prophet everything. How the Prophet kept telling his mother to be careful about this, be careful about that . . .

His voice trailed off. Had he said too much?

Nana's eyes crinkled up at the corners, in the beginnings of a smile, but her voice remained serious. "Be careful, be careful. That takes me way back . . . years ago, to a boy just like you. He lived here in Tamarind Ridge with his mother. I knew them both well. All he heard from her, too, was 'Be careful, be careful.'"

"Why?"

"Remember I mentioned the Forbidden Stream yesterday?"

He nodded. A few grains of rice and beans clung to his greasy fingers. Mum wasn't here. He licked them off.

"We'll be going to the movies later today, but before then, we'll take a walk to the stream to start answering that question. Just to start."

Mum didn't even want him to sit on the sofa. He didn't think she would want him to go to a Forbidden Stream either.

But later that morning, he followed Nana as she trotted down the porch steps. She turned toward the garden. He hesitated, wondering why: the gate was the other way. Still, he followed her along the paving stones, down toward the grave. A pebble broke away from the crumbling edge and skidded out of sight into the deep hole as she trod lightly past. He held his breath, scuttled alongside the yawning hole, and stood beside her on the roots of the neem tree. The roots arched above the ground like writhing snakes, thicker than his waist.

"Feel this, Ato." Nana rubbed his palm over the rough neem bark. "There's power hidden in this tree. Power that could help get you to Nnoma."

She smiled mysteriously at his befuddled expression.

"Next week we'll work together, Ato; I'll help you make a potion."

"A potion?"

She nodded and slipped his arm through the crook of her elbow, leading him back past the grave, toward the gate.

"What kind of potion, Nana? Something magic?"

She laughed and clanked the gate shut behind them. He kept pace with her down the pavement. On either side of the road, sunlight reflected off the walls stretching into the distance. Outside each wall were trim green hedges. They all grew to the same height, as though marked by an invisible ruler. Droplets of water from sprinklers glistened like millions of liquid diamonds on the lush lawns. Gardeners clipped flowering shrubs studding the gardens. And outside every home someone waved and smiled at Nana, or called out a hello, and asked how she was and how lovely it was to see her grandson.

Do they know she has a grave in her garden? he wondered.

The sun was burning directly overhead and Nana's skin glistened with a sheen of dampness. She dabbed her forehead with the loose sleeve of her dress. They were on the edge of an open field where a few children played with balls and rode bicycles. The field was nearly the length of a soccer field, with clusters of shrubs and patches of both short and tall grass. Through it stretched a path, which Nana marched across. As she walked, children called out to her. She gave them a friendly wave back. Ato followed her, the tall weeds tickling his calves. Halfway across, she paused and pointed at something ahead of them on the path. It looked like a strip of old, flattened bubble wrap.

"Snake molt," she said, picking it up. "A green water snake. About three feet long."

His eyes widened. "Can I touch it?"

She handed it to him. "Snakes have got it right, Ato. They leave their old stuff behind and move on to new things. That's something a lot of people can't do."

This was one thing he wasn't going to leave behind, he thought, tucking it carefully into his pocket as Nana walked on ahead.

Soon they were nearing the edge of the field. The grass was a deeper shade of green—there was water nearby.

Nana stopped again, this time by a mango tree. "This tree must have been a cousin of that tree in the Garden of Eden, Ato. For years, it's always had the juiciest fruit around. And look."

Ato followed the direction of her finger. A goblet-sized cluster of leaves cradled in a fork of low branches: a bird's nest. He peeked inside. Three creamy eggs lay in it, barely larger than marbles. All three were cracked.

"They'll never hatch," Nana said. "Maybe the mother bird was killed. Maybe insects raided the nest. Maybe she didn't feel safe. That's why falcons build their nests high up. Few are brave enough to attack a nest there."

Poor bird, Ato thought, trudging behind Nana as she set off again. Was she still alive? Did she make it to safety to build a new nest? He thought about the bird fluttering in the eaves at home. Philomena would drive it off soon . . . if he didn't rescue it first.

He wrinkled his nose. The air was heavy with the smell of rotting.

"You smell it before you see it," Nana said.

The damp earth had dropped away sharply. They were on the bank of a wide stream.

"Behold, the Forbidden Stream!" Nana exclaimed.

He could tell why it would be "forbidden." It was choked with tattered shopping bags, soda bottles, and crumbling takeout food boxes. That was apart from the rotting branches and broken furniture and other things he couldn't make out.

"And over there, that's the Zongo, split from Tamarind Ridge by this stream."

Ato looked beyond the rugged bank, at an expansive sea of rusty tin roofs that extended to the horizon.

"Years ago, when your dad was a boy, many homes there had no toilets. No one picked up their trash. Back then, when the stream flooded, you'd even find the occasional dead sheep floating in here. Things are only slightly better now."

The Zongo was a jigsaw of concrete single-roomed homes built end to end in squiggly lines, wooden kiosks and one-room shacks. He could see where heavy rain had spat into the ground, eating gutters into the red earth around the small buildings. The water had gushed downhill, hacking furrows down the bank, and vomiting their contents into the Forbidden Stream. Children, adults, goats and chickens picked their way nimbly over the terrain. He thought about the straight streets and wavy palms of Tamarind Ridge. Why had Nana brought him here?

"I bet no one in Tamarind Ridge ever came near this stream."

"One young boy did. Someone whose mother kept warning

him to be careful. The boy I told you about. His friends called him BB and he was always playing around this area."

Ato glanced down at the bank, littered with rotting fruit and vegetable peelings. "Why did he come here?"

"Look around. Have a guess."

Ato's eyes roved the banks and then the field. "The mango tree?"

"Correct. His mother had warned him not to climb it. But he did. And he couldn't wait for its fruit to turn yellow. He gorged himself on semiripe fruit until his tummy ached."

Ato laughed aloud. "I do that sometimes."

"The Zongo had no open green space like this field. So some Zongo folk grew corn here. And their kids played soccer here with rag balls. Pretty soon BB had made friends with kids from the Zongo. This upset his mother. At that time, Zongo kids were blamed for a lot of missing stuff in Tamarind Ridge: Clothes and sheets from drying lines. Hosepipes from gardens. Valuables from cars. And now BB was hanging out with them. His mum wanted him to be someone she could be proud of, so her friends could see what a great mother she was. But here he was, hanging about with kids who couldn't read. Who wore dirty clothes . . . and stank. BB's new friendships filled his mother with fear. She was afraid her son would become a vagabond, just like the Zongo kids he was hanging out with. Soon her fear turned to hatred."

"She hated the Zongo kids?"

Nana nodded. "And she didn't want them near Tamarind Ridge. Did you notice the mix of children on the field today?"

Ato nodded.

"That's what she did not want: kids from that side, playing with kids on this side." She glanced at her watch and reached for his hand. "But that's enough said for today. Let's get ready for the movies now, and one of these days I'll take you into the Zongo. Someone there is dying to meet you."

Ato let go of her hand. "Me? Who?"

"That would be telling," she called, already setting off on the path. He hurried after her, casting a final look at the scrum of earthen and concrete rooms that made up the Zongo. Who wanted to see him there? And what would it be like?

CHAPTER SEVEN

◊ ◊ ◊ ◊ ◊ ◊ ◊ ◊ ◊

ATO OBSERVED THE FEAR IN PHILOMENA'S EYES WITH SATIS-
faction. Life couldn't be better. He'd come back from a great
weekend at Nana's, eating all his favorite foods, with trips to the
movies and a museum. Now he also had something that would
keep Philomena out of his closet—forever.

"Philomena, on the first night at Nana's something slithered up
to my door," he whispered. "I'd kept my lamp on, so I could see
the door handle, turning down, s-l-o-o-o-w-l-y."

Philomena gasped and clapped her work-worn hands to her
cheeks.

Ato suppressed a laugh. Philomena had yawned her way
through her Monday cleaning. But she'd snapped awake after he
began telling her about his weekend with Nana. He planned to
give her more than she expected. He had time. His mother had
dropped him off home from school and had gone back to work.
Leslie and Dzifa would be coming over soon, after their homework
was done. Together they would head off to Turo to water and weed
their Nnoma project.

"I called out—Is that you, Nana?"

"Then what?" she breathed.

"Then the handle turned back up s-l-o-o-o-w-l-y. The Thing slithered away."

"Eii! Fire! Fire! Fire! Burn this evil!" Philomena clapped once each time she exclaimed "Fire!" "Ato, you escaped! Have you told your mama?"

Ato shook his head vigorously. The last thing he wanted was Philomena blabbing to his mother about what he'd snuck home. "Shh! You must never mention this. Otherwise . . . otherwise . . ." He tried to think of a suitably horrible consequence. He remembered what she'd told Dzifa. "You'll turn into a tuber of yam."

She gasped. "No!"

He nodded solemnly. "Yes."

"Was the Thing your nana? She wanted to suck out your spirit and breathe hers into you?"

He shrugged. "I dunno what it was. All I know is the Thing kept trying to come in. I kept my eyes open all night. In the morning I found this on the floor outside my door." He reached into his closet and whipped out the snakeskin Nana had picked up in the field.

Philomena toppled backward, gurgling in terror. "Eii! This is bad medicine! Juju! And you brought this magic back here!"

Bad medicine. Juju. He hadn't thought about that. It sounded wonderfully sinister. Philomena was making this more fun than he had planned.

He nodded. "It's powerful magic. I checked it out on Google.

If you tell anyone about this, your tongue will fall out. And then you'll turn into a tuber of yam."

"F-fire! Fire! Fire!" she stuttered in agitation.

"The next day Nana took me to a scary river—with dead animals floating in it."

"Eii! She wanted to throw you in? To sacrifice you to river gods?"

So Philomena believed Nana would do that. Ignorant. Dzifa was so right about her.

"Who knows what her plan was?" He clenched the snakeskin. "But I had this. It protects me, and makes me strong."

"Don't let her take you anywhere strange, Ato," Philomena advised. He was lucky not to have been possessed by that Thing, she added, heading to the cleaning cupboard on the open-air kitchen patio. He would have needed deliverance to rid him of it. She had heard of someone who'd been possessed by a snake spirit. After a severe beating by a powerful Deliverer, he had vomited out six large snakes and fallen unconscious for three days.

For a woman paid to keep homes clean, Philomena did a lousy job with the cupboard, Ato thought, watching her rummage through it. It was a bomb site—a cluster of buckets and mops and crumpled dusters. It was a wonder she found anything in there. He left her to pick out her cleaning items, muttering "fire" under her breath.

Twenty minutes later, he had scribbled out the answers to his homework and was out in front, ready when Leslie and Dzifa arrived.

51

"What's she doing?" Leslie asked, pointing to Philomena.

Philomena stood outside the house, viciously jabbing the handle of her cobweb brush at something in the eaves. It was a scraggly cluster of twigs and dried leaves nestled above their heads. A small bird with dull brown feathers peeped nervously out.

"Philomena, don't do that!" Ato exclaimed, diving toward her. How could he have forgotten that he'd planned to move the nest?

But Philomena aimed her broom handle upward again.

Ato snatched it from her. "What's wrong with you?"

The cleaning woman turned accusing eyes to him. "Can't you see what this is?"

Dzifa rolled her eyes. "Hmm . . . feathers, a beak and wings. Lays eggs in a nest. What were you thinking, Philomena? A hippo?"

"You don't know anything. When people want to spy on you, they send their spirits in the form of animals." Philomena shot a meaningful glance at Ato. "Am I lying?"

Ato ignored her tone. "Leave it, Philo," he said shortly. "We'll take the nest to Turo. You won't need to worry about it from there."

Philomena muttered something about fire and foolish children. She had finished her job and was going to her meeting, she said.

Ato discussed a bird-rescue plan with Dzifa.

Leslie looked skeptical. "I don't know if we should be messing with wild mother birds."

He was ignored.

Ato handed Dzifa an old cardboard box and dragged out a stepladder from behind the kitchen. Propping it against the wall, he climbed up and carefully removed the nest. In it lay four tiny blue eggs. Fine white fluff clung to them. The mother bird fluttered around, circling, diving at them and twittering its dismay. With one clever move, Dzifa had the bird trapped in her box.

"Don't worry, little birdie," she murmured through the closed flaps of the box, following Ato out the gate toward Turo. "We're protecting you."

Ato stepped carefully down the lane, holding the nest aloft. Leslie carried their project book and followed a few safe feet behind. Philomena had marched out ahead of them toward the House of Fire. After every few steps she would turn around and raise a warning finger.

"It's a good thing we're protecting this nest," Dzifa declared. "Birds and butterflies and lizards are literally vanishing from cities and the countryside. Humans are chasing them away."

"I hope we're not going to catch some disease from it," Leslie said. "And I hope if we do go to Nnoma, there won't be an outbreak of an infectious bird or rat disease. Is there a doctor on the island?"

He might as well have been speaking to the breeze.

In front of them the lane forked in two directions, left to the House of Fire and downhill toward Turo. Ato noticed Philomena had stopped at the fork. She had met the Prophet of Fire and was talking to him. Now she was pointing at them. Now the Prophet was giving them a hard stare. Then he was advancing toward them—fast. Ato's steps faltered. Then stopped. Beside him, Dzifa and Leslie halted too.

The Prophet reached them. His arm swung up.

Ato tried to duck. "No!" he exclaimed in alarm.

Dzifa, still clutching the box, dived to defend the nest. "It's just a—!" she shrieked.

But it was too late. Prophet Yakayaka swept the nest out of Ato's hands and onto the lane. The nest scattered apart on the red dirt. The semiliquid contents of the smashed eggs spilled into the dust. Dzifa dropped the box in dismay. The little bird flapped off, twittering forlornly.

The Prophet of Fire pointed at the remains of the nest. "Hosts of Fire, burn the secret agents! Hosts of Fire, burn the enemy! Hosts of Fire, incinerate this!"

"It's not an enemy, it's just a bird! Why did you do that? It hasn't done anything, and now you killed her babies!" Dzifa wailed.

Philomena watched the drama with undisguised relish, muttering triumphantly about people turning into birds to spy on others.

"Ato." The Prophet turned a stern face to him. His finger was in direct line with Ato's forehead. "I've heard about your drawings: scenes of blood and death! Beware—spirits are taking over you." He drew out the *s* after "spirits" as if there were ten of them.

"And you." He turned to Dzifa. "The Spirit of . . ."

Her angry magpie eyes smoldered like coals. Ato could tell she was too furious to speak.

". . . Disrespect. And Defiance. I recognize them. I have cast them out from many children."

Prophet Yakayaka turned to Leslie, who was twisting his fingers in agitation. His gaze softened. "You are a fine boy.

Obedient. Your mother is doing well with you. I will be interviewed in three days, this Thursday, by the nation's biggest TV
station. Wear tidy clothes and come and stand by my side. You
will be interviewed too."

Leslie's mouth hung open, his face a mix of disbelief and
pleasure.

The Prophet's eyes switched back to Ato and Dzifa. "So, you
see, fame is the reward of a child with the Spirit of Obedience."
He turned and strode toward the House of Fire. Ato and Dzifa
stared at each other, aghast. Leslie stared after the Prophet as if
he'd seen an angel.

Choco trotted up to them and licked Ato's hand. Ato knelt and
locked his arms around her neck, burying his face in her fur. He
felt sick and angry, and Choco made him feel better.

CHAPTER EIGHT

◊ ◊ ◊ ◊ ◊ ◊ ◊ ◊ ◊

THAT THURSDAY, NOTHING ATO COULD DO WOULD MAKE Leslie look his way. Leslie stood beside Prophet Yakayaka on the front steps of the House of Fire, wearing his Sunday best and Sunday smile. The Prophet wore a white suit. One hand rested over his heart, the other on Leslie's shoulder.

Dzifa eyed Leslie from her position beside Ato, underneath a shade tree in front of the House of Fire. "Even if you walked on your head he wouldn't look here, Ato."

She was right, Ato admitted. He'd pulled dozens of ridiculous faces, and made several rude finger signs at Leslie. Yet Leslie's eyes had stayed faithfully glued to the cameraman. A group of other people stood on the steps around the Prophet. They were all regulars at the meetings, including Leslie's mother, with her orange handbag. Everyone was dressed to impress—it wasn't every day the nation's most popular TV station popped up in their little community.

The TV crew itself was made up of only three men. The main

man was a reporter wearing a pink shirt and purple pants that were shrink-wrapped around his twig legs. He stood in front of Prophet Yakayaka, asking questions and thrusting a microphone to the Prophet's lips for his answers. It was a warm afternoon—a wet patch was spreading across the back of the pink shirt. Behind him a bored-looking man was filming the interview in between glances at his phone screen. The third, a soundman, fiddled about with microphones, earpieces and the Prophet's loudspeakers. Every sound boomed back over the loudspeakers.

"Good afternoon," Pink Shirt said, looking into the camera. "This is Maximilian Odum from Ghana's number one station, Sunshine TV. We're live with Prophet Yakayaka of the House of Fire on what he calls 'Giving Thursday' to hear about the wonderful work he's doing at Agoro, his home for rescued street children."

The Prophet stroked his mustache and patted Leslie's shoulder. "Children need a safe place to grow," he said, looking into the camera. "That's what I want to give them. A clean, loving home to develop their talents. To feed them—with butter bread and hot chocolate and beef stew and jollof rice with chicken. To clothe them. Teach them. Train them. But all that goodness means a lot of money." His speech turned to how much it cost to feed one child and buy medicines and books and clothes.

Soon Leslie was given the microphone. He spoke about how kind the Prophet was to all children. "Please give as generously as you can so the children of Agoro can have the same chances in life as I do," he ended, with a winsome smile at the camera. His mother looked like she would faint from pleasure.

Ato thought again about the kids in Agoro with no mother and no father. If—the thought was too scary to think about—but if something happened to Mum, Nana would look after him. But some of these kids probably didn't have a nana. It was very kind of the Prophet to help them.

When Prophet Yakayaka began announcing phone lines people could call to give their money to help Agoro, Ato and Dzifa wandered off, to the shady area around the back of the House of Fire. The TV shoot would soon be over, and they would walk with Leslie to Turo to work on their project. Their plants were coming up nicely. By yesterday, barely a week after they'd been planted, all the tender green shoots had pushed up through the soil.

Behind the House of Fire, the weeds and grass grew knee high. Several trees offered both shelter from the sun and a discreet post to view the area—Papa Kojo's straight rows of vegetables, and the pond glimmering like a mirror in the sunshine. Their project was hidden behind the rock, but even from this distance Ato could see more crows than usual hovering around their plot.

"We're going to need a scarecrow," Dzifa suggested to him.

Ato agreed. "I could get old clothes to make one. I'll find something of Mum's from that drawer in my closet. We could make a really freakish scarecrow."

Dzifa grasped a branch from the tree beside them. "Ato,

remember how we used to climb this tree, and play hide-and-seek here?"

"Yeah. This place was just bare walls and no roof."

So much had changed, he thought. Back then, they got into the building by hopping through the low window openings at the back. Those openings were now blocked with grime-covered glass panes. He sat on a window ledge and flicked his pen in the air repeatedly, catching it each time. Dzifa perched beside him. Their conversation moved to Nnoma.

"Life isn't fair," Ato said moodily. "Leslie doesn't even want to go to Nnoma, but his mum is telling everyone how amazing it's going to be for him."

"Why do you care?" Dzifa's small lips curled.

Ato flicked his pen up in the air once more. "Well, it's all I've ever wanted. But my mum has told me not to get my hopes up. I don't think she believes in me."

"Again, why do you care? Your nana's potion will get us there!" Dzifa grinned.

"I haven't said anything about that to Mum," he warned. "And I only told you and Leslie about the grave in her garden. I don't want Mum to know. She'd be bothered about it and tell the Prophet and then he'll start talking to her about being careful and stuff."

"Dummy. You told Leslie. He'll tell his mum. She'll tell your mum. Your mum will tell the Prophet."

Ato grimaced. He gave one flick of his pen. It curved above his head and disappeared behind him.

"There," Dzifa pointed.

It had slipped between the metal frame and the glass window behind him. He stuck his finger in, trying to nudge it out.

"Kinda tight." He pushed on the frame to ease it away from his pen, wincing as a dull pain spread through his neck.

Crack!

Dzifa jumped. "Easy!" But her warning was too late. The latch was broken and the window now rattled loosely in its frame.

"It was a rusty old thing, anyway," he said, fishing out his pen and sliding the window shut. He rubbed his neck. It had felt achy all morning.

"No one will notice the broken latch—not with all these weeds," Dzifa added. "Plus it serves Prophet Yak right for smashing the nest."

They hurried around to the front of the building. Just in time. Leslie had changed back into normal clothes. Prophet Yakayaka was speaking to a couple of members who listened to him with rapt attention. Maximilian was packing his equipment away with the other two men.

"That all looked super boring," Ato said as Leslie joined them on their way down to Turo.

"It was actually very exciting," Leslie sniffed.

Dzifa snorted. "Wow. Saying that with a straight face too."

"Hey, kids!"

They turned around. Maximilian was behind them, with his two team members. "Is there a shortcut here to town?" the reporter asked.

Ato pointed to the track that went past Turo. "That way."

Maximilian grunted his thanks.

"That's going to be a good show on TV, isn't it?" Leslie asked the reporter. "I bet millions of people will watch it."

Maximilian brushed away something from his nose. "Millions of people do what the Prophet does. Not really worth my time, but I need the money."

"But he's helping a lot of poor children," Leslie pressed. "He makes sure they have a clean place to stay. And good food—he gives them butter bread and hot chocolate and beef stew and jollof rice with chicken."

Maximilian cocked his head. "Is that interesting? Are people going to be dying to watch that? It's about relevance. I want my news to be relevant."

"Relevant?" Leslie looked perplexed.

"It means something important that means a lot to people," Dzifa answered.

Maximilian looked at her with interest. "So you're Miss Smart."

Ato pointed at Leslie. "And he's Mr. Goody Two-Shoes. Please, good afternoon, Prophet Yakayaka. Please, please, thank you, Prophet Yakayaka . Yes, please, you may scrape your shoes on my face . . ."

Maximilian grinned.

"I don't do that!" Leslie flashed back indignantly.

"Actually you did, but it looks great on camera," Maximilian winked. "Viewers like to see a polite cherub begging them to help other kids."

"Well, I think Prophet Yakayaka asking people to give money for Agoro is relevant, and lots of people are going to give him money for it. And I have three thousand cedis in my savings account and I'll donate a bit."

Ato rolled his eyes. "Oh yeah, we've heard about your savings for years. You've never taken out a penny of that. I don't think the Prophet's hungry kids will get lucky."

"I will give some money. I have an ATM card. My mum lets me keep it. Because I'm responsible and she trusts me."

Ato made a face. "He doesn't want to hear about your money, Leslie. He wants news."

"Relevant news," Dzifa added.

They had arrived at their project. The emerging seedlings spelled the rising promise of Nnoma. Maximilian's crewmates sat on the rock.

Maximilian seemed to be enjoying their company. "Yeah, relevant. Like when some famous person goes and does something stupid. Scandalous. Secretly doing something terrible. Viewers like to see people get caught for doing bad things. A buddy and I started off together at the same time at Sunshine. One day he got wind of an accountant at a big company who was stashing away company money for himself. My buddy reported on it. Scandal went viral. My buddy is big now. Sunshine Station sends him to report on the mega-stories. And I get sent to the hungry kid stories." He rubbed his fingers together. "I want the big news. The breaking news. I want people to say 'OMG, what happened!' when they hear 'This is Maximilian reporting.'"

"Maximilian is Latin. It means 'the greatest,' " Dzifa said.

"Definitely the brain of the group," Max replied, and raised an approving brow. "You can call me Max."

"And I'm the eyes and ears of the group. I know stuff," Ato said grandly. "I'll keep my ears to the ground. I'll give you relevant news when I hear anything."

"Maybe he wants to tell you his nana is a witch who makes potions and has a grave in her garden," Leslie said peevishly.

"You're just jealous because I know things and you don't because you're too busy sucking up to the Prophet to hear anything relevant."

"His nana is going to make a magic potion from neem to help him get to Nnoma. He's going to be her witch's assistant. You should report that, Max."

Max shrugged. "That's not news, Leslie. There are lots of witches in Ghana. Especially in my old school. All the teachers were witches. Anyways, nice meeting you kids. Gotta go now."

His two crewmen stood up from the rock. As they strolled off, Ato was surprised to feel sorry they were leaving. He liked this restless reporter with the sweaty pink shirt.

Choco was making her way to them from behind the trees.

"Hey, not happy to see me?" Ato rubbed her back vigorously. The dog gave a feeble wag of her tail and sniffed at Ato's hand. She took the bone and flopped onto the ground beside them. Her head rested on her front paws.

"Tired?" Dzifa asked the dog in a tender voice.

The water lilies in the pond had caught Ato's attention. Their leaves were drooping, and a deep circle of yellow had appeared around their edges. They almost looked like they were wilting to death. Don't be silly, he thought to himself, pressing his thumb against the jabbing in his neck. How can leaves wilt when they're standing in water?

CHAPTER NINE

◊ ◊ ◊ ◊ ◊ ◊ ◊ ◊ ◊

THE PAIN HAD STARTED ON THURSDAY, AND BY THE TIME ATO woke up on Friday morning, it hurt to move his neck. Still he packed his bag for Nana's, and dumped it onto the backseat of his mum's car.

Somehow he made it through school. By the time his mother picked him up after classes, the sun had been quarantined behind dark, heavy clouds. It hurt to speak. Not that Mum noticed how quiet he was. She kept (a) glancing at the skies, (b) fretting about making it back home in time for the Friday Fiery Deliverance meeting at the House of Fire, (c) saying she did her best to look after him so there was no need to eat at Nana's as if he hadn't been fed in months, and (d) instructing him to simply answer "she's fine" if Nana asked him how his mother was, because that was the sort of sensible thing to say and his father never said more than he was supposed to.

Ato longed to play his falcon game and soar away from Mum's warnings. He couldn't: the waves of pain from his neck to his head made imagining too difficult. So he stayed slumped in the front seat and dully replied "yes, Mum" to everything, keeping his eyes on her scratched dashboard.

At Tamarind Ridge, Nana was waiting outside her gate. As soon as his mother had driven off, she cupped her hands around his face.

"Ato, you're hot. Where does it hurt?"

He brushed his hand across his forehead and his neck. "Here. And here."

It felt like a big, hard soccer ball was being pumped up in his head. Large drops of rain began to slap at his skin. Nana grasped his limp wrist, led him indoors and bundled him into his bed.

BRAVE SMART SWIFT LOYAL

The peregrine falcon on the ceiling circled slowly within the words. Or was it circling his head? It was hard to tell. He slept and woke. Slept and woke again. He was freezing. Then burning up. Then shivering again. And through it all the soccer ball in his head kept inflating. Nana hovered around like a great formless shadow.

She's got you now. You're trapped. Run, Ato.

He was hallucinating, he knew, but he couldn't help the thoughts in his fevered brain. He couldn't control the pathetic way his limbs shuddered. The front door opened, then shut. She'd left him alone with his terrifying imaginings. The rain pounded a steady rhythm on the roof. Outside his window the wind whooshed through branches with the force of a river.

A flood was approaching. Like the night his dad was born. But instead of being born, he was going to die. He had to be careful. Very Careful. He'd been warned. Nana would push him into the rushing water to sacrifice him. He would be washed into the Forbidden Stream, and he would drown there, along with the sheep. His grave was waiting.

The front door opened again and the roar of storm winds crashed through the house for a moment, then was abruptly cut off. The door had been shut.

Nana was rubbing his shoulders to wake him. His mouth was full of bitter sawdust.

He wanted to keep lying down, to close his eyes, but she wouldn't let him. She was propping him up on a footstool and steam was rising into his face. A pool of dark water formed before him—with floating leaves and branches. She was bending him over, pushing his head down. She wanted to force him in, to drown him. He struggled, trying to fight her off, but her hands were too strong, her dark honey hands that could handle any problem, including a boy who didn't want to die. He whimpered, losing hope, as she draped something soft and heavy over his head. Everything went black. It was hot. She was going to cook him. Steam filled his nostrils, his lungs, he struggled against her, but those strong hands wouldn't let him go. A faint hint of bitterness hit the back of his tongue.

"Shh."

She wanted him to stop fighting. She murmured something about neem.

Neem. Her potion. Be careful of her potions. An ingredient for a potion—that was what she needed him for!

He writhed beneath the dark covering but she was holding him down.

"Breathe in, Ato," she coaxed softly.

Breathe into you, Philomena had said . . .

He bucked feebly, trying to throw off the heavy cloth.

"Shh, shh." And she was stroking his shoulders. Her whisper sounded like the rustle of breeze through leaves. "Breathe in. Breathe out. Breathe in."

There was no fight left in him, so he breathed in . . . and out . . . and in . . . His pajamas were clinging to him. Gentle hands replaced them with dry ones. A warm hand caressed his forehead . . .

. . . and he was the falcon, gliding over the dark water, rising, soaring up into the midnight sky . . .

♦ ♦ ♦ ♦ ♦

He blinked. The darkness had been chased away by sunshine. He clenched his toes over the ledge at the top of the mountain, stretched his stiff wings and looked around . . .

"There you are." Nana sat on a stool by his bed. Behind her, the sun shone warmly through the voile curtains. Her hands were curved around a bowl with a spoon sticking out of it. "You must be hungry."

He was, he realized, stretching his sore limbs and struggling to sit up in bed.

The fragrance of cooked millet meal with cloves and spices tickled his senses. He scooped up the porridge eagerly. It was hot, smooth and sweet, easing energy back into his weakened frame. It didn't take him long to clean out the bowl. Nana was back with a second helping. That too went down fast.

She stretched her legs out on the low stool and smiled. "A friend brought it this morning."

"The same friend?" His voice sounded raspy.

"Yes, I told him you were unwell."

Ato paused with his spoon in midair. "Him? I thought your friend was a woman."

"We all assume a lot. Now let's get you washed and settled for a restful day in bed."

Nana was a good nurse and a fun companion. All Saturday she stayed beside him while he slept. She chatted about hunting birds with him when he woke, ate alongside him and improved his fever with her steamed neem leaf vapors.

That night he slept soundly and deeply, and by Sunday morning he was sitting on the sunny porch—his first time outdoors since he'd arrived two days before. His head felt clear, the ache in his neck, throat, arms and legs had disappeared. It was a fresh morning, with the air washed free of dust by the rain. The garden sparkled a pristine green.

He sat across from Nana. On the porch table between them

was a heap of leafy neem stems. His easy task was to pluck leaves from the stems and drop them into a basin. Nana grabbed handfuls of these leaves, grinding them into a thick green paste in an earthenware hand mortar she had set between her feet on the porch floor. She had winked cagily when he asked what they were making, and had instead picked up the story about BB.

"BB. That's an odd name for a boy," Ato remarked.

Nana shrugged. "That's what he was called. And BB became very attached to a particular boy in the Zongo. I remember his name—Yusuf, skinny lad with a curved nose. Looked like a rake. When BB's mother went out, he would sneak Yusuf into his home. They would race in the garden, bounce on the mattresses and have pillow fights. BB let Yusuf play with the expensive toys his mother bought him. He had quite a range of toys. I remember a particular water pistol. Impressive. I used to watch BB shoot at objects with it from fifty yards away."

It was just like Nana to remember some kid's water pistol from way back, Ato smiled, separating the stems from the plucked leaves.

"One day BB's luck ran out. His mother came home early. There was BB, with his Zongo friend Yusuf, who had his feet up on her precious furniture. What was worse, BB was eating oily bean cakes that Yusuf had brought, and Yusuf was eating the sandwiches BB's mother had made him for school. And Yusuf was playing with BB's water pistol."

Ato's thoughts flashed to his mother. He dumped a handful

of leaves into the basin. "I can imagine what happened next," he grimaced.

"She drove Yusuf out of her house."

"Yup, that's what I thought."

"Then she stormed across the field, and over the bridge. Yusuf had fled to his mother, who was washing clothes near the stream. BB's mother marched right up to her and warned her not to let her boy come near her home ever again. She said Yusuf was taking her son's good home-cooked food in exchange for filthy Zongo food."

Ato winced. "That sounds horrid." He thought about his friendship with Dzifa, and how often he'd heard his mother and Leslie's mother call her "wild." It would be awful if his mother ever banned him from talking to her.

Nana mashed harder at the green paste, wielding the hand pestle deftly, crushing every leaf. "Well, Yusuf's mother got mad. Told BB's mother that BB wasn't any better than Yusuf.

"Yes he was, BB's mother shot back."

"Noooo! That sounds so wrong!" And also sounded like Leslie's mum, Ato thought.

Nana scooped out the paste into a larger bowl and stirred water into it from a bottle beside her. "Things got nasty. A bunch of other Zongo mums joined in and a yelling match began. BB's mum was outnumbered a dozen to one. As she was leaving, she threw them a warning: she would have a fence built across the field to keep their scruffy Zongo kids where they belonged—in the slum."

She handed a thick wooden spatula over to Ato and gestured to him to stir it some more. He did. It looked like spinach soup. With a bit of string, Nana secured a muslin square over the opening of another bowl. She poured the green soupy liquid over the fabric, and sat back to watch the liquid filter slowly through the fabric into the bowl.

Nana rinsed her hands over a flower pot. "For a few weeks BB didn't go anywhere near the stream. But as the saying goes, 'Return to old watering holes for more than water; friends and dreams are there to meet you.' One day he decided to test the waters—literally. He crossed the Forbidden Stream. Sure enough, Yusuf was on the other side. But he wasn't alone. There was a whole crew of other Zongo boys too. Their mums had told them to shun BB. They said he'd told his mother stories about Zongo kids stealing food. BB had to scramble across the stream back to safety. War had been declared and his friendship with Yusuf was as dead as the Forbidden Stream itself."

Ato felt a pang of sympathy. "BB must have been super upset."

"He was. Blamed his mother for losing Yusuf as a friend and moped about for days. His mother was happy to have gotten rid of those pesky children, though. She began urging the Tamarind Ridge residents to build the wire fence to keep Zongo kids out. And she warned her son to be careful of Zongo kids and never to go near the stream again." Nana paused and smiled. "But the devil had planted temptation by the Forbidden Stream. Guess what it was."

"The mango tree?"

"Indeed. One day, BB slunk down there to pluck some mangoes. He had his water pistol tucked into his shorts. While he was up the tree, the boys on the other side saw him. They leapt over the stream and dashed to the tree, whooping. BB scrambled down and ran. But he dropped something."

"His water pistol?"

"Exactly. The Zongo boys snatched it up and scampered back off with it, whooping and cheering."

"Oh no!" Ato groaned. "That must have killed him!"

"It certainly did." Nana rose. By now, only leaf mush remained on the fabric. She squeezed out the last few drops of green liquid from the muslin square into the bowl. "Ato," she announced with a smile, "your organic plant pesticide is ready."

CHAPTER TEN

◊ ◊ ◊ ◊ ◊ ◊ ◊ ◊ ◊

THE FOLLOWING AFTERNOON, ATO FOUND A FROG LYING ON the muddy bank of the pond. Its pale underbelly was exposed, its limbs outstretched. It was dead. Close by in shallow water, another frog floated, just as dead. The next day, Tuesday, he noticed a lizard twitching on the rock nearby. It didn't move even when Dzifa nudged it with a stick. Not far from it was a bird on its back, with its legs stiff in death. By Wednesday, four fish floated upside down in the pond, gills splayed open.

On Thursday, Ato and his friends gathered at Turo to weed their project, water it, and build their scarecrow. Though crows continued to swoop too close to their tender sprouts, Ato noticed something else: some smaller birds in the shrubs seemed too sick to fly off, even when he drew close to them. Choco too lay quietly beside them. And she had not yet touched the bone Dzifa had brought her.

Leslie took a picture of a tiny brown sparrow with his phone. It was huddled on the ground, shuddering and blinking slowly. "It's some animal disease," he said, before picking up his watering can and heading off one last time to the standpipe.

"It's more than an animal disease," Dzifa said, looking around. The reeds growing in and around the pond had all lost their firmness, and leaned limply to one side. Most had turned a sickly straw color. A number that had begun curling up the week before were completely shriveled. The leaves of the water lilies had all turned yellow and brown.

Something was wrong at Turo.

Despite all this, their project was looking more exciting each day. They had sprayed all their plants with Nana's pesticide. It was more powerful than their black soap; not a single bug or aphid was in sight and their plants were growing better than expected, too. If they could convince Papa Kojo to switch from his sacks of chemicals, then their Nnoma chances were good.

The big problem, though, was that, across the pond, Papa Kojo's was not a good story. Together with his sons, he tramped up and down between the rows of vegetables. They stooped to inspect the leaves and had pulled up some to scrutinize the roots for worms. For the first time Ato could remember, Papa Kojo had not smiled back when they'd waved at him. Neither he nor his sons stopped to stare at the House of Fire behind them, where another Giving Thursday was going live on TV, in front of a crowd, with Max brightly visible in his tangerine-orange shirt.

Papa Kojo might not have enough produce left for them to compare their vegetables with, Ato sighed.

"It's weird that your nana used neem leaves to cure you, and the same neem leaves to keep bugs away from plants," Leslie said, finally done with his watering job. "Maybe it is a magic potion. We could give the animals here some of your nana's neem potion to heal them. Your mum wouldn't like that, though." He selected a stick to form a gnarled arm for their scarecrow.

Ato made a face. His mother's lips had tightened when he'd mentioned Nana's leaf steam medicine to her. He'd thought she would have been glad. Instead, he'd later heard her from his room, on speakerphone with Prophet Yakayaka. He'd heard her say it was no wonder his father had died. Indeed, the Prophet cooed—Ato had escaped great danger.

Dzifa looked up from the dried coconut that would become the scarecrow's head. "Ato, you were sick. You got better. I don't get what your mum was upset about." She set the scarecrow's head on the stuffed sack of grass that was its body. Ato knotted a bright orange and red scarf around the scarecrow's neck. It was a lucky find among his mother's giveaway stuff in the bottom drawer of his closet.

"It could be a slow-working evil potion. Nothing happened to you at first, but after a few days you might start growing scales or something," Leslie offered helpfully.

"That's not how spells work," Dzifa said, fingering the scarf. "Witches and wizards are busy. They can't hang around for days waiting for their spells to work. They mutter a spell. There's a puff of smoke. Then, where the person used to be, there's a toad on the ground, and a warm pair of shoes."

A burst of clapping from the House of Fire made them turn. The Prophet of Fire was on the steps of the House of Fire. Several large shiny cars were parked in front of the building. Over the loudspeakers, announcements blared out of lavish gifts coming in for Agoro—hundreds of cartons of tinned food and supplies, and several very large checks.

Leslie beamed. "I bet when people saw me last time they were just dying to give money to help the children."

"And how much have you given for the children?" Ato asked.

"I came on TV for them, didn't I?"

"That cost you nothing. So it means nothing." Dzifa cast him a sweeping look of disdain.

"It cost my time. Time is money."

"That's our Leslie," she teased. "Tight as a nut."

Leslie rammed the scarecrow post into the soft ground. While the clapping and giving went on in the background, they put the finishing touches on their scarecrow. When they were done, Ato stepped back to inspect it.

"Woah!" he breathed.

All disagreements were forgotten as they admired their creation. Holes gouged into its coconut head were eye sockets. Shreds of red plastic had been stuffed into these holes. Matchstick teeth were glued into another cavity below its eyes. A pair of twigs stuck out as arms. Broken combs were tied to the end of each twig, like mutated fingers. Empty milk cans swung from string attached to the twig arms, clinking in the breeze. Best of all was the red and orange scarf. In the breeze, it billowed out like the wings of a burning angel. The crows had all flapped away and were squawking their alarm from the safety of the trees.

Dzifa rubbed the scarf again. "Ato, are you sure your mum didn't want this?"

"What did I say? Everything Mum puts in the bottom drawer of my closet gets given to poor people. She'd be very happy I got rid of it for her."

In the distance, Giving Thursday was over, and Max was coming their way with his two vacant-eyed crew members.

"Hey," Ato waved.

Max waved back cheerfully, picking his way over the ground, avoiding muddy patches.

"Wow!" He took in the scarecrow with its gaudy scarf flapping madly in the breeze. A hollow, tinny chorus rang out from the milk cans. Choco seemed to have found her strength and had courageously launched an attack on the edge of the scarf, leaving one corner tattered.

"Planning to give the wildlife nightmares, eh, kids?"

Dzifa folded her arms proudly.

"Any news apart from you kids obviously watching too many horror movies?"

"Yeah, there's news," Ato said gravely. "Something's wrong here. Things are dying."

The other two men wandered ahead, but Max hung back to listen in amusement. "Dead frogs. Dead birds," he replied. "I guess that counts as news around here. Gotta run, though. Call me when you have something worth my time. I'll be back this way again three weeks from today, on the sixteenth of April. It's going to be a grand Giving Thursday; big day for Mr. Prophet. Lots of VIPs coming to that."

"Yes, I'll be beside him that day too. He needs me. That's what he told my mum," Leslie chipped in.

Ato rolled his eyes at Leslie and whipped out his pen from his pocket. "Can I have your number?" he asked Max.

Max rattled off his phone number. To Ato's chagrin, his pen had run out of ink. Leslie came to his rescue, and triumphantly tapped Max's name and number onto his phone.

"I'll call you when we figure out why things are dying," Ato said. Max chuckled as he ambled off with his team. Soon they disappeared through the trees.

At the House of Fire, all the boxes were being packed away into a large truck. Soon it drove off, and the Prophet was making his way down toward them.

"I hope he doesn't come here," Ato said. The last time, the Prophet had made him feel uncomfortable about being at Turo.

"I hope he does," Leslie said.

The Prophet had paused to speak to Papa Kojo. Papa Kojo's normally level voice was hoarse and agitated as he gesticulated toward his vegetable lots.

"I been awake all night now, Prophet. I can't sleep. I been so worried. Everytin' I plant is dyin'."

Prophet Yakayaka knelt on one knee and touched the ground

with slim fingers. He closed his eyes and was motionless for several moments. Then he opened his eyes. They were clouded with concern.

"There is evil beneath!" his voice rang out.

Papa Kojo and his sons exchanged looks of alarm.

Ato felt an apprehensive tingle. Dzifa stood in silence beside him. Leslie's mouth had formed a horrified and silent O.

Prophet Yakayaka's troubled look deepened. "I have felt it in my dreams. Now I feel it in this place: a powerful force, a deadly spirit that I have not encountered before. It is seeping from the earth's core, up to our water and our land. There are powers at work. This is not a safe place. I will try to defeat it by fire. But not every battle can be won." He straightened up and looked toward Ato and his friends.

Ato could tell from his face that he had seen their scarecrow. But the Prophet was looking at it too closely. Now he was making his way through the grass to them. The Prophet marched up to the scarecrow and gripped the scarf.

"Children, where did you get this scarf?" His eyes traveled over all three of them.

"It's an old thing my mother . . ." Ato's voice trailed off. He suddenly wasn't sure whether his mother had really meant to give it away. Dzifa flashed him a what-did-I-say? glance.

Prophet Yakayaka's voice was soft. "I gave this to everyone who came to the Fiery Deliverance meeting. Did your mother give you this—to put on a scarecrow?"

"It was in my drawer."

"Did she give it to you?"

"She put it with stuff she doesn't want."

For a long, loud moment, there was silence.

Prophet Yakayaka's eyes narrowed. "Spirit of Defiance. Spirit of Mischief. Spirit of Destruction." He sounded as if he could not believe so many spirits could fill one twelve-year-old boy.

Ato felt shame crawl all over his body.

◆ ◆ ◆ ◆ ◆

That evening, he was banished to his room. "How could you have taken the scarf without my permission?" his mother had clucked heatedly. "You've embarrassed me. And shamed your father's good name. I nccd you to stop misbehaving and get good grades in school and make me proud so everyone can see I'm bringing up a gentleman, not a wild child!"

She was on the phone to Prophet Yakayaka that night. Yes, she agreed with him: Ato was becoming quite mischievous. Yes, he was possibly being influenced by that wild child, Dzifa. And yes, his grandmother too. Here, her voice dropped. Yes, grandmothers had Strange and Powerful Spirits. Yes, something had to be done about it. And yes, there was something evil in the area around Turo. The children would have to be very careful.

He got into bed and shut his eyes tightly. It had all gone so wrong, he thought miserably. He'd never seen her wear anything that went into the bottom drawer. It was unfair that Dzifa was getting blame thrown at her; she'd actually warned him about using it. And Nana—what did she have to do with anything? It was all too hard to figure out. He pulled his sheet over his head and tried to think of a flying falcon. The only image that formed was one of his father holding a flapping red scarf and looking reproach- fully at him. This isn't good enough, Ato, he seemed to be saying.

CHAPTER ELEVEN

◊ ◊ ◊ ◊ ◊ ◊ ◊ ◊ ◊

"EVIL BENEATH? THAT'S WHAT HE SAID?" NANA'S DARK EYES narrowed thoughtfully.

Ato burped and nodded.

Their breakfast was long over but the aroma still lingered on his breath and fingers. He had enjoyed their routine: breakfast of spicy waakye and then a chat on the porch while the morning sun was still high. Nana sat on her sofa, he on the cane chair across from her. She had listened closely to his worries about what Prophet Yakakaya had said. Would the evil beneath Turo hurt him, or his friends? What about their project?

"Mum is scared now, Nana. She thinks something might happen to us in Turo. This morning she said there's more to life than going to Nnoma."

A lump formed in his throat. "But going to Nnoma is all I've ever wanted." It wasn't fair. Their lettuce was growing fast, the okra, spinach and spring onions looked so healthy.

"All these years Turo has been fine, Nana. Why did this evil stuff have to appear the year Nnoma opens? Now I'm scared something will happen to our project, like Papa Kojo's vegetables. And he keeps talking about spirits in us. It's scary."

Nana pulled her slim legs up onto the sofa and clasped her knees to her chest. Her purple and yellow tie-dyed skirt draped down softly, covering her toes.

"He speaks about spirits in you. Indeed, spirits are powerful, Ato," she said. "They can be like horses, wild and harmful: horses can knock you over, kick you and drag you where you don't want to go. But when horses are controlled, they can be helpful—carrying you safely wherever you need to go. Spirits are like that—helpful or harmful."

"Spirits can be helpful or harmful," he repeated slowly, trying to make sense of her words.

She realized his confusion. "Take the Spirit of Fear, Ato—one of the most powerful spirits of all. Think about it: What stops you from getting too close to a cobra? Fear. That's when fear is helpful—when it can save your life. But fear could also make you scared of a rope, because it looks like a cobra. That's when fear becomes harmful, like a wild horse, tossing you about, making you scramble everywhere. And some people will swing a rope in your face. And you think it's a cobra so you . . ."

". . . run."

"Exactly. In the direction they want you to."

Ato remembered his illness the week before, and how scared he'd been of what Nana might do to him. And all the time she was healing him. He remembered how much he'd loved her garden when he was little—and how years later the same garden seemed to close on him like an enchanted trap. He was confused about everything. His mother was scared and nervous about a lot— including Turo. Once she heard about the evil seeping up in Turo, she might even want him to drop the project.

"I don't want to forget about going to Nnoma, Nana. I want to keep working on our project. Should I be afraid of that, the evil beneath Turo?"

Nana leaned forward. "Think about your cassowary, Ato. It could have run. It could have forgotten that it was brave and strong enough. But it didn't. And it also didn't forget what it had—a secret weapon. It didn't forget who it was—a cassowary. Remember, Ato, what you are—smart and swift, brave, and loyal to what you believe in." She fluffed out her skirt around her legs. "Fear makes us act in a way that can make us ashamed of ourselves later. Remember BB?"

He nodded.

"Well, his mother went around driving the Spirit of Fear into us Tamarind folk. She told us how the Zongo kids would teach our Tamarind children to steal and drop out of school. How we had to protect our kids from the Zongo folk. I was scared. I had only one son. Pretty soon nearly half the Tamarind Ridge residents wanted that fence built across the field. They decided to put it to a vote. BB's mother needed enough people to agree with her to make a majority. But someone stood in her way."

"Who?"

"Someone who thought the Tamarind Ridge folk were unkind in their treatment of the children. His name was Mr. Bempong.

The Zongo kids were children, he said. When kids were left to themselves, they naturally ran wild, he said. Like all children, they needed attention and a firm hand. Mr. Bempong had a plan. He went around telling people about his plan, convincing people not to vote for the fence. Pretty soon, the votes were split."

"What was his plan?"

"That's something you'll find out this afternoon, when we get back from the city raffia fair."

◆ ◆ ◆ ◆ ◆

Much later that day, when the sun had begun to travel toward the Zongo in the west, Ato found himself again following Nana down her street to the field. Instead of crossing it toward the Forbidden Stream, Nana turned left onto a skinny lane that snaked along the top edge of the field. The lane led to a little bungalow with curtained windows and a porch facing the road. It was the last house in Tamarind Ridge, closer to the Forbidden Stream than all the other homes. A dwarf wall circled the house, marking off its yard. They stopped at the wooden gate beside a lemon tree that twisted its way into the air. Within the square of short grass and flowery shrubs that made up the yard stood a garage with open windows. Inside, about a dozen children sat at wooden desks, listening attentively to a tall man, old but erect, thin as a whip, standing at a whiteboard. His gray head faced the board, pointing out something to the children.

Ato looked curiously at Nana. She sat on a cracked concrete slab facing the house, and he settled down beside her.

"That English-language instructor has lived here over forty years," Nana said. "When he first moved here, he would stand by this wall and observe the Zongo boys pushing carts and playing in the Forbidden Stream instead of attending school. And then he heard about BB's mother trying to win votes to put up a fence that would keep them out. So he went around Tamarind Ridge asking people to help him get the young Zongo minds into reading and writing. Not only that, he went over to the Zongo and convinced the mothers to let their kids come over to study in his garage for a few hours every Saturday. That was his plan."

"You mean that's Mr. Bempong?" Ato looked at the older man with fresh respect.

"Yes. And the Zongo kids swarmed to his lessons." Nana smiled. "I figure the orange juice and cookies he gave them at the end of each lesson were the bigger pull. Nonetheless, he plowed on. He was determined to make a difference in their lives. Mr. Bempong did not believe in mixing work with play. In fact," she chuckled, "he did not even believe in play unless it was a crossword or Scrabble. He would read aloud to the Zongo kids and get them to read back to him. They learned poetry and read adventure and detective stories. And he had a very firm hand. It was the only place in the estates where the Zongo children felt completely safe. I think that was why BB's ex-friend Yusuf decided to take the water pistol there one day."

Ato raised his brow.

Nana nodded. "It was a bad idea. BB had friends. Those friends saw Yusuf take the water pistol into the class."

Mr. Bempong looked up and waved at them. Class must have just ended because the kids scraped back their chairs and began rising from their desks. They each picked up a paper bag at the door and trooped past Nana and Ato at the gate, a mix of boys and girls, all smiling and waving at Nana.

"Thank you, grandma."

"Good afternoon, grandma."

"Bye-bye, grandma," they called.

Some had already fished out small cartons of juice and little meat pies from the bags. Ato wondered why they were thanking her. She knew their names too, calling out a couple and asking about their parents.

Mr. Bempong walked out to them with a stiff, upright gait. His gray beard was clipped close and his head revealed a smooth bald patch surrounded by a half circle of short gray hair. He looked like a man whose smile would be hard to win. Nonetheless, he smiled at Nana, showing perfectly set teeth.

"Serwa!"

Nana tapped Ato's shoulder. "My grandson, Ato," she beamed.

Mr. Bempong pumped his hand several times, warm and hard. "I've been looking forward to meeting you, Ato. Haven't seen you since you were this high." He touched a hand to his hip.

The Zongo children were doing well, he told Nana. One of them had been short-listed for an essay prize in the capital region.

"Thank you for the snacks you supply them, Serwa. It keeps them regular to class!"

The children's cheerful thank-yous and greetings suddenly made sense to Ato.

"I was just telling my grandson about Yusuf, and that day years ago with the water pistol," Nana said.

Mr. Bempong raised an eyebrow to her. It seemed to Ato that he was asking a question. Nana gave an almost imperceptible shake of her head. Surely a man this old wouldn't remember that story, Ato thought. He was surprised when Mr. Bempong nodded, resting his hands on his hips.

"I can never forget, Serwa. That day, Yusuf's desire to gloat far overshadowed his sense of caution. While he sat cockily in my class, I saw a boy approach from the gate." He turned to Ato and grinned. "You see, I'm most interested in boys when they are in the classroom, but I'll excuse you today. I strode outside to the boy and sternly asked what his business was."

"Was he scared of you?" Ato asked.

"I could see he was. I did not like interruptions of any kind. Privileged Tamarind Ridge boy randomly walking in to disturb Zongo kids during their lessons." He shook his head disapprovingly. "Such a child would be made to sit in the back corner of the garage with a finger over their lips. Or would stand facing the corner in front of the class. The wise Tamarind Ridge child stayed away from my home on Saturdays.

"Yusuf has a water pistol, the boy said. It's not his, he said. He stole it! I gave him a hard glare. A stolen toy? In my garage?

Yes, the boy said. Maybe you should search their bags, Mr. Bempong."

Mr. Bempong hesitated. "It occurred to me that the boy might have been playing a prank. I know what children are like; if their imaginations are not directed into essays and poetry, they think up strange and silly things. I warned the boy—if he was trying to get Yusuf into trouble, he would regret it for a long time. I instructed him to stand outside the gate, then I walked back into the garage. Stand up behind your desks, I ordered the boys. Confess, I said. There was silence. I asked once more. Then I began to search them. Sure enough, I found it—in Yusuf's bag. At that point Yusuf snatched the water pistol from me and fled toward the stream."

Mr. Bempong patted his trim waistline. "Ato, in those days I could still run one hundred meters in twelve seconds. In a few strides I had grabbed the rascal and hauled him back to Tamarind Ridge. By now a number of mothers and children from Tamarind Ridge had emerged from their homes. Yusuf was a thief, they shouted."

Ato held his breath. He wouldn't want to be in Mr. Bempong's clutches now, much less back when he'd been in his one-hundred-meters-in-twelve-seconds prime.

"Yusuf was in my grips, and a handful of mothers and children followed us shouting loud and angry comments, a pack of hounds baying at a scared rabbit. He was a skinny boy, always barefoot and wearing shorts a couple of sizes too big for him. The sleeves of his T-shirt hung way past his elbows. The owner of the water pistol, BB, trailed very slowly behind them all."

He glanced at Nana again. Again she smiled and shook her head.

"I handed the water pistol over to the boy's mother. She grabbed it and asked her son, 'This is your water pistol, isn't it?'"

"BB's mother was terrible, wasn't she?" Nana asked Mr. Bempong.

"Simply awful," he chuckled.

"And then what happened?" Ato asked, eager to find out more.

Nana lifted her gaze across the field toward the Zongo and drew him close. "We need to leave Mr. Bempong now, but next week we'll cross the Forbidden Stream. Someone will tell you what happened next."

They said their goodbyes to Mr. Bempong and headed off home.

"Who's that someone in the Zongo, Nana?" Ato asked again.

But all he got back was a mysterious smile.

CHAPTER TWELVE

◊ ◊ ◊ ◊ ◊ ◊ ◊ ◊ ◊

ON SUNDAY EVENING, MUM SCRUTINIZED HIM CLOSELY. SHE asked dozens of questions too. What did you do at Nana's? What did you eat? Where did she take you? She searched his face as if he was keeping something back from her. She watched his every move. When she called him into her bedroom to ask yet another question, he understood why she was acting so strangely: a slim, printed pamphlet lay open facedown on her bedside: *Signs of Possession by Spirits*. By Prophet Yakayaka.

He felt like a goldfish in a bowl, and to make himself feel better, he focused his thoughts on their project for Nnoma. All weekend he'd worried about it, hoping their plants were all right, safe from the evil seeping up in Turo. He asked his mother if he could go over to have a look. Her reply was swift and sharp: No! Not in the dark! He was too obsessed by that project. And anyway, he had to accept that he might not even get into Nnoma; other kids probably had better projects.

Not long afterward, his luck broke through. His mother had a headache and asked him to be quiet while she rested for half an hour. When he peeked in on her ten minutes later, her chest was rising and falling gently in sleep. She clutched the Prophet's pamphlet as if she feared someone would snatch it in her slumber. He softly clicked her door shut.

Two minutes later he was trotting down the road toward Turo. Be quiet, she had said: it didn't get much quieter than not being home at all, he thought. Heavy cloud had blanketed the moon and the road was dark.

The House of Fire was closed and silent, but he avoided the path leading to it. It would be just his luck to have Prophet Yakayaka meditating on his front steps and seeing him whiz by. He took the long way around instead, skirting behind the nighttime food stalls further down his road. Most people were indoors. A few hopeful sellers had set up their stalls and lit them up with fluorescent hand lamps that threw out light a few feet around them. The smell of food filled the air—bread and fried eggs with tea, noodles with vegetables, and the sweet-sour smell of steaming kenkey.

He skipped across the road and disappeared into the grove of palm nut trees. They offered him welcome protection from the view of the locals. There was something in the air—a crisp, charged atmosphere. Electricity, he had heard his teacher describe it. And that smell of oncoming rain; Dzifa said it was the smell of ozone from high up.

He made his way through the trees that bordered the back of Turo and arrived at their project. Going down on his knees, he examined their plants. His heart lifted. Every one of them was fine—spinach, okra, radish, lettuce, spring onions and corn. In fact, they were growing faster than they had expected. Nana's neem spray was truly a magic potion. And the ground was moist—Leslie had watered it over the weekend. He inched a couple of feet further to inspect the last row of corn . . . and stumbled over something warm and solid.

Heart thudding, he sat back on his bottom. What was that? Then awareness rushed through him. He could see now—a form he recognized well even in the dark: Choco! He scrambled forward and stretched out to touch the dog. She was lying on her side. Grasping her head in both hands, he stroked her muzzle, shaking her gently. Why was she lying here? She gave a barely audible whimper and licked his hand weakly.

"Choco." He shook her more urgently, rubbing her fur. The tip of her tail twitched. He lowered his face to hers, so close he could feel her shallow breaths. Her eyes were half closed. Her rib cage heaved up and down. What was wrong with her? Had she eaten something bad?

"Choco." He brought his lips close to her ears. "Here, girl. What's wrong?" He tried to stem the crippling panic and helplessness rising in him. The evil, from the core. It must have seeped into her, just like it had done with the frogs and birds and lizards. How could he stop it? A knot tightened in the pit of his stomach. What was he supposed to do now? It was so late! At least she was still breathing.

He pressed her all over, checking for bumps, a broken leg perhaps, but there was nothing, no whine of pain. The wind tugged at his T-shirt and the smell of rain filled the air. He couldn't leave her here to get soaked. Besides, somebody might kick her and hurt her some more. He picked her up. She was heavier than he expected. She didn't resist, just lay limply in his arms.

Where could he take her? He thought for a second. Maybe he could carry her over to Papa Kojo's. No. His mother would hear of it, and he was supposed to be doing something quiet—at home. It occurred to him that she might wake up any moment and realize he was missing. Things would really be bad then. He had to get back quickly.

Then he saw it right beside him: the rock. Of course! He could lay her in the shelter of the ledge underneath it. He set the dog down and scrabbled around in the dark gathering plantain and mango leaves, spreading them on the stony ledge. Gently, he lifted her and settled her there. She would be safe from the rain. "Please be okay, Choco," he whispered into her ear. "Just rest here. Tomorrow we'll get you help."

Water, he thought. He'd heard of dehydration, and how it could kill. Maybe she'd been lying here a long time and a drop of water would revive her. He cupped a plantain leaf and hurried to the pond. Just as he lowered his hand to the water, he heard a voice. No—voices. Low voices. He shrank back. Two forms materialized, silhouetted in the darkness. Whoever it was hadn't seen him. He shrank back up the path, and stumbled over a pebble. He froze. The voices fell silent. One form melted away. The other shadowy form remained—standing still. Had they heard him?

He flattened himself beside the rock. Whoever it was didn't want to be seen; and neither did he. Footsteps approached. Ato could hear his own breathing, loud as wind in a tunnel. The shadow continued its approach.

Slowly. Stealthily.

Crunch.

Crunch.

Silence.

Then Choco whimpered. A second later a face appeared in the dark, inches from his.

Ato stared into Prophet Yakayaka's eyes.

"You." The Prophet's voice was low and hard.

For a moment there was no sound except their breathing. Then Prophet Yakayaka spoke, his lips so close his breath tickled Ato's ear.

"What are you doing here? Have you any idea what evil lurks here at this time? Or are you here to do evil? To join forces with agents of darkness? To dance with evil spirits?" After each question he paused, before asking the next.

The Prophet wrapped a cool hand around Ato's wrist. By now Ato's breath was trapped in his chest.

"Spirits of Mischief. Playing with you, boy. Drawing you where you should not go. Can't you say 'no' to the temptation of the spirits whispering to you? Do you not know they can take on any form, even pretend to be a dog, just to lead you to your doom?" He traced a line with his finger across Ato's forehead. "I must draw them out, Ato. I must deliver you."

A shiver tingled through Ato. He wanted to flee, but there was someone else out there. Someone who might catch him, or hurt him.

"Please . . . it was the dog . . ." His throat ached from fear.

"Does your mother know you're here?"

"Umm . . . I . . . I . . ." He knew his quavering voice had given him away.

"Maybe I should call her and tell her." Prophet Yakayaka's hand slipped toward his pants pocket, reaching for his phone.

"Please!"

The Prophet's nose brushed his.

"Go straight home," he ordered. "Leave this place!"

Someone was still out there, in the shadows. Ato ran. He ran all the way home, the wind and his blood rushing through his ears. He eased the front door open and slipped in. The house was still in darkness. Cautiously and silently, he pushed his mother's door open. She was still asleep. The pamphlet had slid from her hands to the floor. Back in his bedroom, he switched on his lamp. Only then did he notice his pants and shoes were covered in purple prickles. His mother would be annoyed. He would have to sort it out later. He tugged them both off, tiptoed to the kitchen, dumped them in a black plastic shopping bag, and stole out to the kitchen patio. Philomena's room was in darkness. She would be fast asleep. Quietly, he opened the cleaning cupboard and shoved the bag at the back.

Raindrops began to spatter down. He slunk back to his room, changed into his pajamas and slipped into bed. His chest hurt from the drumming of his heart.

CHAPTER THIRTEEN

◊ ◊ ◊ ◊ ◊ ◊ ◊ ◊ ◊

ATO'S MOTHER STOPPED TAPPING AT HER CALCULATOR AND studied him. She had brought him home from school that afternoon and was staying behind to attend the Monday meeting at the House of Fire. Mondays were quiet at the shop.

"Why are you so fidgety, Ato?"

Because last night while you slept I snuck out to Turo and Choco was very sick and I don't know if she's better and I don't know whether Prophet Yakayaka's going to tell you he saw me there.

Dzifa could probably have told her mother that. Scratch that: Dzifa could probably have pulled her mother along with her to Turo last night, and taken Choco back home with her. He stopped kicking the leg of the dining table and extracted his badly mauled pen from between his teeth.

Tat-tat-tat. Her fingertips drummed the stained wood tabletop. "Are you nearly done with your homework?"

"Yes, Mum." In truth, instead of finishing his French homework, he had drawn dot-dash-dot lines at the top of his sheet and poked holes in the middle of it. His thoughts were on the night before at Turo. At school that day, he'd told Dzifa and Leslie about it. Dzifa had said a prayer for Choco. Leslie had reminded him how much trouble he could have gotten into if his mum had woken up and found him gone.

He scratched out answers to the past tense of *penser*. Choco had probably just needed a rest, he reassured himself. Maybe she'd been dog-tired from running around. He smiled at his play of words. Two French verbs to go. Philomena had entered the room with her bucket and duster and was wiping the dust off glass louvers. She yawned with every other swipe over the glass. He itched to point out the corners of the glass she kept missing, but that would be a dead not-paying-attention-to-homework giveaway, so he forced his attention back to his sheet.

A vision flashed into his head—people on the point of death who'd been revived by one sip of water. How he wished he could have given Choco that drink of water! Water was life; he'd heard that time after time. Maybe last night's rain had dribbled onto the ledge and she had lapped up a few drops. And maybe some of that electricity in the air had charged her up, like a phone plugged into a socket. Yes, she would be feeling better. He had saved a chicken wing from lunch—not just the bone, the whole wing. She'd love that.

He filled out the remaining gaps on his sheets, with no attention to correctness. On the stroke of 4 p.m., he shoved his work into his bag and untruthfully replied "yes" when his mother asked if he'd read over his work. By the time he stepped outside, Philomena was on their tiny porch cleaning the fly netting.

"Ato, are you going to Turo?" She looked as if he were heading out to take a swim with a shark.

His mother was still within earshot. He touched a finger to his lips.

Philomena frowned. "You should not go. I would never go there if I were you. Never."

"Last time I checked, you weren't me," he muttered. And he was off, flying down the middle of the street leaping over the muddy potholes, and swerving onto the lane that led past the House of Fire. Ahead of him was the rock and Papa Kojo's rows of vegetables. Then he was at the branch in the lane where Papa Kojo and his sons were standing in a half circle with their backs to him. They were not on their side of the pond. They were on Turo. Why? And why were they looking down? What were they looking at?

Another step forward and he saw Dzifa—in the center of that half circle, squatting on the wet earth, on her knees. She was digging her fists into her eyes, crying. In front of her, on the ground, a small mound of leafy branches concealed something. He didn't want to see what it was. He knew. His eyes were already burning. His head was burning. His fingertips were burning. Papa Kojo turned a pitying look to him. No one spoke, until he forced himself closer and saw Choco's brown snout sticking out from beneath the leaves.

"Why did she die?" Dzifa voice was shaky with her sobs. Snot streamed from her nostrils.

Papa Kojo placed a sympathetic hand on Ato's shoulder. Ato felt the scalding force of tears gathering behind his eyelids.

A few local people had seen them and walked over, curious and disturbed.

"The dog, she looking sick to me all of last week," Papa Kojo's son said.

"It's a bad sign," another person said. "All of last week, frogs, fish, mice. All dead."

"First de vegetables, de plants, den small animals and now de dog," Papa Kojo said.

"Next thing it will be people," his son said. There was heavy silence after that.

Leslie was approaching. His feet slowed as he took in the scene. A few feet away, he stopped.

"Did she die?" he asked.

No one answered, but he still gave a small cry and clapped a hand over his mouth.

"We have to bury her." Ato's lips felt wooden. Tears dripped down his chin.

Leslie recoiled. "Do we?"

Dzifa whipped her head up, twists flying. "You want to just leave her here, Leslie?"

"Don't yell at me." Leslie raised both hands. "We don't know what she died of—some contagious disease or something. Black plague from rats."

Dzifa muttered something that would have earned her immediate detention had they been in school. One of Papa Kojo's sons produced a spade. The whole group moved away from Turo to the area behind, where trees took over the shrubs. With Leslie and

101

Dzifa standing by, Ato took the spade and shoved it into the soft ground. But his tears blinded him. His inexperienced arm shook. The spade wobbled in the ground.

Papa Kojo's son took the spade and began to dig. His muscles rippled and glistened as he quickly and efficiently scooped out a grave, about two feet deep. He turned toward the dog, but Ato was already bending over Choco, brushing away the branches. He slid his arms underneath her.

She was really dead.

The awful reality paralyzed him. No, he gritted his teeth. He would carry her to her grave. He would do this one last time for Choco. One step at a time, he carried her over, and laid her gently in her grave. She just fitted in it. He remembered her chicken wing. Retrieving it from his pocket, he laid it by her snout. Leslie sniffled. A fly settled on the dog's lips. Dzifa swatted it away with a small branch.

Papa Kojo's son began to shovel earth over the dog. With each spadeful of earth that landed on her fur, Dzifa's sobbing grew louder. Ato allowed his tears to spill freely down his cheeks. He'd never seen an empty grave before this year. Now he'd seen two . . . because he'd been afraid and he'd run away and left Choco. She had died. Alone. In the dark. If he'd taken her home, or to Papa Kojo's, she might have made it through the night. His shoulders shook with grief.

By the time the sorrowful task was completed, they had company. Prophet Yakayaka was passing by before his 5 p.m.

meeting at the House of Fire. Papa Kojo, his wife, sons and a few locals clustered around him, shaking their heads, pointing to their vegetable lots and to Choco's grave, and muttering fearfully about bad things going on.

This was not good, the Prophet said repeatedly. His tone was terse. The evil was here. It was rising and spreading. It had to be stopped. The people needed to join him to call down Fire on the evil. They could set the evil alight in another realm and destroy it, he declared. They might even have to sacrifice this place to save the whole area. There was much nodding and murmuring of agreement, and soon they slowly dispersed in various directions. The Prophet was left standing where the earth sloped to meet the pond.

He beckoned Ato over to him with a crooked finger. Ato covered the short distance between them hesitantly. Placing his hand under Ato's elbow, the Prophet steered him a few yards away from his friends.

He folded his arms across his chest and looked straight into Ato's eyes. "My dear boy, do you see what is happening? You are a channel. You have brought death to the dog."

Ato stared back at the Prophet. What was he talking about? Him? A channel? To kill Choco? Because he had run away? He tried to speak, but all he could manage was a weak "Me?"

Prophet Yakayaka nodded.

Ato looked around wildly. Had anyone heard what the Prophet had said? It didn't seem so. Leslie stood, still sniffling, scrubbing his hands with sanitary wipes. Dzifa was on her knees, placing a small bunch of field flowers on Choco's grave. Prophet Yakayaka looked at him with a mixed expression of disgust and sorrow.

"We heard from Leslie's mother that your grandmother has a grave in her garden. You drew a picture of a dead dog. So it had to become reality. Now you have a dead dog. In a grave. Death and graves followed you. Do you see the power of the spirit in you? It creates things from what you have seen, from your thoughts and actions. The evil in this place has found a channel through you. Deliverance is the only answer. But"—he raised a warning finger—"you must stay away from this place."

With that he turned around, striding up to the House of Fire.

Ato's lip quivered. He bit down on it—hard. His thoughts were a mush of confusion and fear. Could it be true? Had Choco died because of him? He'd drawn the evil to her. And then he'd left her alone . . . alone with whatever dreadful thing was here. Did anyone else think he was a channel? Why did Leslie have to tell his mother about the grave? He walked back slowly to his friends, trying to keep his face blank so they wouldn't know . . .

Dzifa searched his face with puffy eyes. "What did he say?" Her voice was thick with grief.

He sniffed and rubbed his eyes vigorously. How could he tell her it was his fault Choco was dead? This was a nightmare, and he wanted to get away from it. He crouched on the ground and shut his eyes, but all he could see was a falcon flapping jerkily, unable to get off the ground. Falcons were hunters, predators, but for the first time he felt like the prey, the one who needed to escape.

CHAPTER FOURTEEN

◇ ◇ ◇ ◇ ◇ ◇ ◇ ◇ ◇

TUESDAY MORNINGS HAD ALWAYS BEEN TOUGH. FORCING himself to concentrate during Biology, History and French lessons normally required all his willpower. Now it was impossible. Ato couldn't forget the feel of Choco's stiff body in his arms, the sight of her in the grave—tail motionless, legs still forever—just like his drawing. The sound of the spade scraping into the ground, and dirt scattering over her body, echoed in his head. And it was his fault. He'd drawn a dead dog and now Choco was dead.

By the fifth lesson of the day, Art, he was sent out of class for writing DEAD all over his sheet instead of shadowing the block letter E, as the teacher had instructed. Out in the corridor, he comforted himself with the thought that there was surely a heaven for the spirits of good dogs. Then the word "spirit" sent a shudder through him and he wondered whether anyone in his Art class was going to die because he had written "dead" several times on his sheet. Because maybe the Prophet was right: he was a channel.

When the bell rang for the second break in classes, he scuttled off to the bathroom and hid in one of the toilet cubicles. Alone in the stuffy enclosed space, he flipped down the toilet lid, sat down and rested his head on his hands. On the back of the door someone had scribbled some rude words with a black marker about a girl and boy—the kind of writing that got all the kids into trouble and drew long talks on Decency and Decorum from the headmistress at assembly. Sounds of kids shrieking on the basketball court drifted in through the small, high window—kids without a care because they weren't channels for evil spirits. He looked down glumly at the dull red floor tiles.

Outside the cubicle, boys shuffled in and out of the bathroom. Water splattered noisily into the sinks, and someone skidded on the wet tiles. A few times there was impatient banging on his door. He kept silent and lifted his feet onto the toilet seat so they wouldn't show under the door. Twenty-five minutes later, the bell rang. The break was over. As soon as he emerged onto the corridor, he came face-to-face with Dzifa.

"I saw you come in here. I was waiting for you." She looked at him searchingly. "You took so long."

He could no longer bottle up what Prophet Yakayaka had said. Everything tumbled out in a jumble of hushed sentences while his eyes darted around to be sure he wasn't being overheard. He could not be known as the kid with the killer spirit.

"I'm scared now, Dzifa," he finished miserably. "Scared of myself. When I shut my eyes I see horrible things happening to people I care about, and then I get more scared because I'm afraid those things will actually happen. Just because I saw them in my mind. Because I'm a channel."

Dzifa stared at him. "A channel? Do you believe him, Ato?"

"I don't know."

The second bell rang. He ran to his next class, leaving Dzifa staring after him.

After school she made a beeline for him.

"Ato." She grabbed his arm. Her tone was urgent. "I can't shake it off. What if Prophet Yak is trying to scare us, to put fear into everyone?"

"Why would he do that?"

. . . fear could make you scared of a rope, because it looks like a cobra . . . And some people will swing a rope in your face. And you . . . run . . . in the direction they want you to.

Nana's words ricocheted through his head above the melee of noisy school kids around him.

"Ato," she said, "he says you're a channel. It doesn't mean it's true! And I'm not saying this just because my mum called the police on him. I know your mum and Leslie's mum and everyone else around here thinks the sun shines out of his armpits. That's fine. But what if he is just trying to scare you? To scare us? Why? Why does he want to scare us?"

"Because he wants us to run?" Ato spoke slowly and uncertainly.

Dzifa stared at him. "You've got some working brain cells. That could be it. He wants us to run. But why?"

Ato's brain cells clicked and whirred like a rusty toy. He shook his head in frustration. "Search me."

"No. Search him."

"Huh?"

"Maybe he is trying to keep us away. He wants us to run away from Turo. Maybe there's something he doesn't want us to find out. Maybe he stole some money and buried it there or something. Maybe he even buried somebody there."

"But why is everything dying there now, since our project began?"

"I dunno," Dzifa confessed. "And yeah, that's scary. But there must be a reason and I don't think it's a Spirit of anything."

Ato's mind was calming down. He felt like a falcon that had finally taken off from the ground after struggling to get away. He was not running away anymore. He was flying, a hunter chasing his prey. His decision was swift and instinctive. "We should have a look around, Dzifa. You know, starting from the House of Fire." A light flashed on in his head. "Remember that window I broke? Maybe it hasn't been fixed yet. We could slip through, tomorrow even. It's Wednesday, it will be quiet."

"Wow. From zero to a hundred!" Dzifa's face lit up with admiration. "Let's go for it, Ato! Prophet Yak might have something there, or written something down . . . all those books he carries around. My mum says if something's rotting under the bed, we might not find it, but there'll still be a smell."

"I'm not coming," Leslie announced when they shared their plan with him later that afternoon at Turo. He doggedly gave all his attention to the flourishing plants, walking to and fro with his watering can, taking pictures and meticulously spraying every leaf with neem leaf solution.

"Leslie, all we're asking you to do is to stand guard," Ato said. "One day when people wonder what happened to those two kids who disappeared in the House of Fire, I hope you'll be able to shrug and get back to your phone."

"I hope you can live with yourself, Leslie Quaye. I hope you can live with yourself if there was something you could have done and you didn't, and you watch us being buried like Choco over there . . ." Dzifa's hands were on her hips, elbows sticking out like coat hangers.

Eventually their efforts paid off, and the following day Leslie stood behind the House of Fire sweating profusely and fiddling with his phone. Behind him Ato and Dzifa slid back the broken window behind the building. It creaked back on its rusty frame.

Leslie looked up from his phone. His eyes were round and agitated. "It says here the penalty for breaking and entering is—"

"Yes. We'd love to know how many years we're going to jail for because you were reading the law to us instead of standing guard," Dzifa snapped.

"Hide. Don't stand there looking like a flagpole," Ato hissed. "And remember, if you see or hear anyone coming, tap the window frame three times."

Leslie crouched down among the weeds, almost fully horizontal, muttering his misgivings.

Ato slithered through the window after Dzifa. They landed in a small room with a rough concrete floor. Old boxes had been stacked against the wall, along with brooms, dusters and a broken trash can. The air was thick with the smell of dust and concrete powder and floor cleaner. Heavy black cobwebs drifted down from the ceiling rafters, trailing along the unpainted wall and clinging to their heads and faces. The door opened out into a narrow corridor, one that Ato recognized instantly. This was where they had played pilolo, years ago when the House of Fire was still an empty, half-completed building. Three doors were set in the wall along the narrow corridor. Right at the very end was a larger wooden door—it led into the main hall, he realized.

"No point looking there," Ato whispered.

Dzifa nodded in agreement. They tried the smooth brass handle of the first door. It turned easily, opening into a room about twenty paces across.

Ato looked around—a mirror on the opposite wall, a shiny wood veneer wardrobe, a polished desk and chair, a plush rug. A couple of glass paperweights rested on documents on the desk. On their right, the entire wall was taken up by a giant poster of the Prophet. In his cupped hands he cradled an orange ball of fire.

Between the wardrobe and the desk was a large yellow plastic four-gallon container. Dzifa was already twisting it open. It contained a viscous liquid, a greenish-blue color—like the ocean. They sniffed it. It smelled vaguely sweet, yet sharp and acidic.

"Is it a cleaning liquid?" Ato asked, screwing the cap back on. "It's an odd place for Prophet Yakayaka to keep it."

The Prophet's eyes seemed to follow him from the wall. "We really shouldn't be here, Dzifa," Ato whispered, feeling increasingly uncomfortable.

"You think?" Dzifa was already sliding open drawers.

Ato swung open the wardrobe door and rifled through the suits, jackets, shirts and the rows of shiny shoes all in black or white with silver buckles.

There was nothing suspicious in the wardrobe. They turned their attention to the desk, setting aside the paperweights and flicking through the sheets beneath them. One of them was a large brown envelope. PRIVATE AND CONFIDENTIAL was stamped across it in red letters. They exchanged glances, shrugged and opened it. It contained a number of sheets of paper. Ato pulled them out. Nothing of interest, he realized. They were several of the same drawings—copies of what looked like colored computer sketches of a building with land around it showing roads and trees.

Dzifa picked up the sheet on top. "I know what this is. It's a building plan. My mum is always working with drawings like this." A second sheet was attached behind with a paper clip. The second sheet was titled PROJECT FUND-RAISING PLAN BY AGORO. Beneath it was a list of dates, mainly Thursdays. A large sum of money was printed next to each date. She flipped the top sheet back in place, laid the drawing out on the desk and looked closer. "This looks interesting."

It didn't to Ato. He replaced the rest of the sheets in the envelope.

"Look, there's the street that leads to our houses," Dzifa pointed out. "And here's the House of Fire. Down here, that's the pond. Is that a bridge over it? And why are there cars at Turo? She frowned and looked closer. "What's wrong with this map?" She tapped at a spot on the sheet. "Look what's missing—right here."

They exchanged puzzled glances.

"That's so weird," Ato muttered, looking closer at the drawing.

"Stop making that sound," Dzifa said suddenly. "It's annoying."

"What sound?"

"That tap-tap-tap—"

"I'm not—"

Realization slammed into them instantaneously: Leslie!

Ato gasped.

Click.

A door had opened.

They froze, exchanging horrified looks. There was nowhere to hide. They shoved the envelope back under the weight. Ato stuffed the sheet in his hand down his shirt and darted out the door into the corridor, with Dzifa behind him.

"Hey!" the Prophet roared from the open door leading to the hall. "What are you doing here? Come back!" They had already raced back to the small room, their entry point. Leslie's frightened eyes stared back at them. Footsteps pounded down the corridor after them. There was no time to climb out. Survival mode kicked in. Ato shoved the drawing out of the window to Leslie.

Leslie snatched it and vanished.

A millisecond later Prophet Yakayaka stood in the doorway. His face was contorted with anger. "You! I will . . ." He raised both arms as if to snatch them both up.

Ato and Dzifa shrank against the cobwebbed corner.

He seemed to change his mind about physically mauling them.

"Out!" he bellowed. He pointed back out to the corridor.

They scurried past him.

"Raise your arms, little thieves! What do you want here? What have you stolen?"

Ato winced as the Prophet frisked their cowering frames and delved into their pockets.

"I will have you arrested for Breaking and Entering! For Burglary! What have you taken?"

"N-nothing," Ato quavered.

"I'm calling your mothers! Sit there!"

They huddled together in silence on the floor of the corridor. Fifteen minutes later, Ato's mother flew in. She was followed immediately by Dzifa's mother, who was wearing ripped denim shorts and a tank top that stopped just above her belly button.

Dzifa's mother took her in both arms. "Darling, are you all right?"

"Your child is an uncontrolled rogue," the Prophet said coldly.

"No negative words in front of my child, please," Dzifa's mother chided. "You'll damage her self-esteem. This is simply a childish escapade. Come, Dzifa. Let's take a walk back home and you can tell me why you're here."

With a final sympathetic glance at Ato, Dzifa scuttled off after her mother.

No such luck for him.

Ato stood with his head hanging and his hands clasped behind his back while his mother clucked her dismay. She agreed with the Prophet; he had indeed warned her. The Prophet spoke darkly about Breaking and Entering, Spirits of Mischief and Disobedience and Havoc, and Nana's Strange Spirit that was leading Ato to Indiscipline and Channels of Undesirable Spiritual Activity. There was only one thing to be done for Ato, they both agreed: Deliverance.

CHAPTER FIFTEEN

◊ ◊ ◊ ◊ ◊ ◊ ◊ ◊ ◊

THAT NIGHT ATO WAS BANISHED TO HIS ROOM. "STAY THERE and think!" his mother fumed, thrusting his dinner around the door. "Think about this disgrace you bring to me and to your father's good name!"

From his refuge beneath his bedcovers, he shivered while pondering the situation. The thought of anyone knowing they had taken the drawing was so frightening, he felt like throwing up. Breaking and Entering sounded bad enough. Taking something was Burglary.

Was he really a channel? Had the spirits made him want to search the Prophet's office? What else would they make him do? Why did they want to live inside him? He wanted them to go away.

He tried to shut his eyes, to sail away on his falcon wings, but all he could see were mischievous, imp-like spirits, writhing like smoke around his wings, pinning them down. Did he really need deliverance? It sounded like a horrible thing, from what he'd heard. His tortured thoughts kept him awake for hours, but he eventually fell asleep.

The next morning he emerged wearily and cautiously from his room, ready for school. On his face was what he hoped was an expression of deep remorse. It did little to help him. His mother's feelings had heated to a simmering rage. There was no "We can't be late today" or "That shirt is crumpled." Instead she gripped the strap of her handbag as if she wanted to sling it at him.

"Your father would turn in his grave, Ato. His son—a vagabond. Breaking and Entering. That's how criminal behavior starts. You're trying to get into Nnoma; your father helped build Nnoma and he got chosen to do it because of his fine character. Now just look at his son. You'll never get in at this rate!"

A wave of mortification surged through him. His father had really been mistaken about him, thinking he was good enough to follow in his footsteps.

"You will be delivered from whatever is taking hold of you, Ato. Tomorrow."

Tomorrow? Friday? He gave a squeak of protest. "B—but I'm going to Nana's!"

She rapped the top of the dining table once with her palm. "Not this weekend." And she fluttered into the kitchen to pack their lunch, leaving her bag on the table, along with her car keys— and her phone. His vision zeroed in on it.

Without thinking, he grabbed her phone. His fingers swept down her contact list. There it was: Nana Serwa. He could send her a message. No. Typing would take too long. Mum was still in the kitchen. The fridge door opened and thudded shut. The cupboard door creaked open. He tapped the call button. Silence.

More silence. He cursed the sluggish network speed and then—
drrr drrr drrr . . .

"Hello, Mina!"

A flood of relief washed through him on hearing Nana's voice, light and cheerful.

"Nana, it's Ato," he whispered hoarsely. "Tomorrow can you please co—"

From the corner of his eye he saw a blur. He whipped his head around. The phone was seized from his hand.

His mother glanced at the phone, shot him a look of fury and raised it to her ear.

"Hello? Ato?" Nana's voice over the phone was clear.

"Nana, this is Mina. Yes. Good morning. I'm very well, thank you, Nana. Forgive me, Ato must have been messing around with my phone. He didn't realize he had actually called you." Fake laugh. "Yes, of course. I'll see you tomorrow then."

And he knew she was lying because it was the same voice she put on when Nana asked her if everything was okay and she said "yes" when in fact she'd been fretting over her calculator for hours before.

She tapped off her screen and slammed the phone onto the table.

"You've changed . . . since you started going to Nana's. I wish I'd never . . ." She stopped speaking, snatched up her car keys and left the room. He followed her to the car. Mercifully for him, Leslie's mother phoned as they got into the car.

Yes, his mother told Leslie's mother, of course she was not

surprised that Leslie hadn't allowed himself to be dragged into following Dzifa and Ato's terrible behavior. Yes, Ato needed more time with Leslie and less time with Dzifa. She was a terrible influence. Yes, that was true, her mother simply did not control her enough.

Ato inhaled and exhaled and shut his eyes. He was a falcon needing a peaceful place. His sturdy wings lifted him, carrying him out the window, sailing on the unstable air currents, once again not sure whether he was the hunter or the hunted.

◆ ◆ ◆ ◆ ◆

It was a relief to be in school, surrounded by dozens of kids arguing and gossiping and teasing each other about test scores. For a while, it took his mind off deliverance and channels and dead dogs. And then, during the first break, he went to the computer room to do some homework "research" and looked up "deliverance."

Bad idea.

Spirits really hated being thrown out of the bodies of people they were living in. He gawked at images of people chained down to stop them from hurting other people while they were being delivered. Would he have to be chained? Some spirits had the power of ten men, he read. On one website, an irate spirit threw a woman to the ground, where she writhed and snarled and foamed at the mouth like a mad dog. He clicked off the computer and sat sweating behind the blank screen.

At the second break, he was unable to eat his lunch, and shared his deliverance anxiety with Dzifa.

"Just tell your mum you won't go," Dzifa offered unhelpfully. "She can't exactly carry you there herself—you're too big."

Ato sighed unhappily. Dzifa sometimes forgot how different their mothers were.

The topic shifted to the drawing, and he agreed with her that it was a very odd drawing and they would take it from Leslie so she could show it to her mother. Her mother could examine it and explain it to them.

But Leslie did not agree with them. "We should not have broken into the Prophet's office. That was so wrong!" He shook his head as if he wanted to fling away the very memory of their shameful behavior from his mind.

"Just give us the drawing. Then you can pretend you never went there. And we'll forgive you for being such a lousy lookout," Dzifa said.

Leslie refused. "It's not your property," he cheeped. "You had no right to be looking at it or wanting anyone else to examine it or anything. I'm going to find a way to put it back. It's bad enough that I have the drawing in the first place. I haven't even looked at it since I got it. I'm praying it will disappear. In fact, the only reason I haven't torn it up is 'cos I'm afraid Fire will burn me up if I do. And I was a good lookout. I began tapping like you said very early, you just didn't hear me because I was tapping softly. Or did you want me to bang on the window like a drum and get caught too?"

Ato took in a deep breath to stop himself from pushing Leslie to the canteen floor and sitting on him until he gave back the drawing. "Leslie, how are you going to put it back without Breaking and Entering . . . again?"

"I'll find a way," Leslie said in a tone that made it clear he had no idea how he would find that way.

Ato would not give up. He followed Leslie into the library.

"Leslie, we've already broken in and we've already taken it, so we may as well have another look it. Perhaps we saw wrong. We can help you put it back, and we'll never argue with you again, 'cos you're right a lot of the time. Just give me the drawing."

Ato was driven out of the library by the librarian, who had no patience for school kids refusing to maintain silence in that space.

At Turo later that afternoon, as they measured their lettuce, Ato felt rising unease about his deliverance the following day.

"I don't want this deliverance thing," he muttered moodily, staring at the ground instead of writing down figures.

"It's prob'ly not such a bad thing to be delivered," Leslie said soothingly. "That day you broke into the House of Fire, you both sounded possessed. Maybe you and Dzifa both need deliverance. Otherwise the spirits might continue to make you do worse things. And I heard that the longer spirits stay in you, the more powerful they get. And then they invite their friends in, and next thing you know, seventy evil spirits possess you. There was this movie where a priest came with a cross and garlic to throw an evil spirit out of someone and the spirits threw the priest around the house. Like a Frisbee. Then they chucked him out of the window. And a car ran over him."

Ato's stomach heaved.

Dzifa turned on Leslie. "Do you even care how Ato feels, standing there listening to rubbish talk like that, Leslie Quaye?"

An argument broke out between Leslie and Dzifa.

Ato kept breathing to calm his surging insides, focusing on dousing the okra and radishes with neem leaf spray. He did not have a Spirit of anything, he told himself over and over again. No matter how much delivering the Prophet did, no mischievous spirits would be found lurking in him.

CHAPTER SIXTEEN

◊ ◊ ◊ ◊ ◊ ◊ ◊ ◊ ◊

AT DAWN THE FOLLOWING DAY, ATO WOKE UP IN A SWEATY terror. A rush of thoughts cascaded over him, each just as horrific as the other. Would the spirit attack the Prophet? Being driven out generally made them bad-tempered. Maybe it would rush out of him like a tornado and on its way out whirl Prophet Yakayaka out of the window like a ball at the end of a chain. His stomach constricted. Would it turn on anyone else? Mum? He went cold at the thought. An image formed of his mother sprawled on the floor like a twisted rag doll. He'd be known as the kid with the killer spirit. He'd have to run away. He shook his head to drive the awful thought away.

No, he didn't want to be delivered. Maybe if he asked nicely, the spirit would leave politely. "Hey, Spirit," he whispered aloud, "are you inside me? Would you, umm, like to find someone else to live in? I know a couple of people." In reality he had no idea who the spirits could go to, but he figured this was a start. He listened intently for a reply from inside. All he heard were birds twittering their morning greetings outside.

There was only one place he could go, he decided as daylight crept into his bedroom. He stuffed a T-shirt and shorts into his school bag. He could squeeze through the thick hedge at the back of the school playing field, change out of his uniform, and hitch a ride to Nana's. She would protect him.

His mother must have read his mind. "Pack some books," she ordered when he stepped out of his bedroom, school shirt tucked in and belt buckled. "You'll work from the shop today."

"But . . . but . . . I have a French test!" he wailed.

"I've spoken to your teacher. You'll take it on Monday before class."

And it did not make a difference when he told her about the other important lessons he would miss.

"Oh, so *now* lessons are important to you?" She rammed jollof rice, chicken, and shredded cabbage into two Tupperware tubs for their lunch. "Do you know what's important to me, Ato? You crossed the line. You crossed the line when you broke into the Prophet's office. It's important to me that you never do that again. Ever." And that was that.

His mother's shop was on the main street close to the bustling Kaneshie market, where she sold fabrics. Women came in to look at swaths of white lace for weddings, and black and red fabrics for funerals. Years ago she had been the only fabric seller there. Now there were several other shops up and down the road. In between customers, his mother sat at her counter and tapped at her calculator, refolded bales of cloth, and rearranged fabric draped over the faceless mannequin in her display window. And once in a while she would cluck softly about what a pity it was that Ato had never known his father and what a good example his father would have been to him.

Through all this, Ato sat at the little wooden chair and table behind her counter, fragmenting into a twitchy mass of terrified nerve endings.

At four thirty she locked her shop and he endured the short, painful drive to the House of Fire in early evening traffic. She parked her car beside the big sign of the Prophet and took him by the hand up the steps. The wind tugged at the hem of her gray dress with tiny blue flowers, whipping it against him. Was that really the wind . . . or was the spirit warming up? Sneaking into the Prophet's office had seemed like a great idea before, but now, walking through the open wooden doors of the House of Fire with his heart crashing against his ribs and people already gathered, he was not so sure.

Straight ahead of them, at the top of the aisle, stood Prophet Yakayaka, with a microphone in his hand into which he growled, "Fire, fire, fire!" When he saw them he nodded. Ato looked away.

A good number of people were already in the hall, about sixty or more, all on their feet. Their loud singing filled the room. They clapped in rhythm. Some had closed their eyes, others clenched their fists, and many more were pacing up and down in the spaces around the seats. Leslie's mother stood with both arms raised. Her deep purple bag took up the seat beside her. The two women exchanged this-is-the-right-thing-to-do looks. Their seats were too close to the front, Ato thought, shuffling reluctantly toward the chair next to his mother.

Above him the ceiling fans whirred like angry little windmills. Glowing white bulbs glared down from metal chains fixed to the ceiling. He shifted from one foot to the other. He laced his shoes twice. His shorts were suddenly cutting into his stomach.

There would be powerful deliverances that evening, Prophet Yakayaka announced. Deliverances from tormenting spirits!

"Fire, fire, fire!" the audience murmured enthusiastically.

The Prophet beckoned to a man in the second row, who stepped forward. His khaki pants were gathered around his waist in folds and held in place by a belt. Prophet Yakayaka gestured to three men standing behind him. They strode forward and stood behind the man with oversized pants. The clapping and chanting in the hall dropped to a low hum. Ato wondered whether this spirit needed to be coaxed out with lullabies, like a baby who needed to be sung to sleep. In spite of the ceiling fans, sweat trickled down his temples. He brushed it away with clammy hands. A lady took the microphone and held it to the Prophet's lips.

"Our brother is tormented by the Spirit of Poverty!" the Prophet declared, gripping the man's shoulders with both hands.

The crowd murmured sympathetically.

"This sinister agent of darkness has poked invisible holes in this man's pocket! All his money drops out magically. The spirit has tied invisible bandages around this man's hands. Every penny he touches slides off his palms. He is getting poorer and poorer. But we say, Enough is enough!"

"Enough is enough!" the people shouted with clenched fists and foot-stamping.

The impoverished man nodded his head vigorously.

Ato wondered what the Spirit of Poverty would do. Would it come tearing out holding bags of cash, viciously hurling them at everyone and knocking them unconscious?

"No more holes!" the Prophet roared.

"No more holes!" the people shouted back.

"Hosts of Fire, seal the holes in his pocket!"

"Seal them!" they shouted.

"Hosts of Fire, burn the bandages!"

"Burn them!" they roared.

"To ashes!" The Prophet hopped in circles. He ground his teeth and stamped on the stage. Perspiration ran in rivulets down his throat.

Prophet Yakayaka placed both hands on the man's head. "Get out!" he roared. "Burn by fire, fire, fire! Get out!" At the last "Get out," he shoved the man violently backward.

The man toppled backward and was caught by the three men behind him. He was stretched on the ground faceup where he lay quite senseless.

Ato's stomach turned to liquid yogurt.

"Fire! Fire! Fire!" the Prophet yelled over the body.

"Fire! Fire! Fire!" the people roared back.

The three men heaved the poor man up from the floor. His arms dangled limply by his sides. One dusty shoe slipped off his foot. As he was lugged to the back of the room, the people in the room clapped and chanted, "Fire! Fire! Fire!"

Prophet Yakayaka wiped his dripping brow with a large red

handkerchief. He turned to Ato's mother and gestured for her to bring him forward.

"No," he whimpered, but his mother half dragged him to the front.

The Prophet closed his hand around Ato's forehead. His grip was firm. Ato squeezed his eyes shut and clenched his teeth.

"This boy is tortured by multiple spirits! They have him in chains. They drag him where no child should go, to do what children should not do."

The crowd murmured their disapproval at the spirits' activity.

"The spirit"—there was an audible drop in the Prophet's voice—"makes him scheme and plot . . ." He fell silent. His grip on Ato's forehead slackened.

What? Had the spirit come out already? Ato opened his eyes a crack. The Prophet was looking over his head . . . at something in the aisle behind Ato.

Ato turned his head slowly, terrified of what he would see.

Nana stood halfway up the aisle, framed against the open doorway. "YOU! Take your hands off my grandson. AT ONCE!" she commanded.

CHAPTER SEVENTEEN

◇ ◇ ◇ ◇ ◇ ◇ ◇ ◇ ◇

THE HOUSE OF FIRE FELL SILENT. EVERY EYE LATCHED ONTO Nana as she strode up to the front. A thousand butterflies fluttered chaotically in Ato's stomach. She took his trembling hand in her warm, strong hand. As he walked back down the aisle on his wobbly legs, the door seemed a mile away. Everyone on either side was staring at them.

His mother hurried out after them. "I had planned to bring Ato over later," she said to Nana. Her voice was high-pitched and panicky.

That wasn't true, Ato thought bitterly.

Nana's look was stony. "Mina, as soon as I heard Ato on my phone this morning, I knew you weren't going to bring him."

"Nana, the Prophet is only doing this to help Ato behave better! Do you know what Ato did? Breaking and Entering!"

"Behave better? Not this way, Mina." He recognized that trace of sadness in Nana's tone from the day she'd told him about his father's birth on the couch.

"It was to help Ato," his mother insisted, now sounding half upset and half apologetic.

He dived into Nana's front seat, slammed his door and locked it. His head was bowed. He didn't want to look at his mother.

For what seemed like fifty years, Nana and his mother stood outside the car talking. He couldn't hear their exact words, since the car windows were rolled up, but gradually he could tell his mother's voice was calming down. Eventually Nana waved her goodbye and sat in her driver's seat. As they drove off, Ato saw his mother standing forlornly outside the House of Fire. He didn't look up or wave to her because blinding tears had filled his eyes and had begun spilling down his cheeks. Only then did he realize how terrified he'd been, at the front of the hall with his head clamped between the Prophet's fingers. Nana steered her car with one hand and clasped his hand with her free hand.

"It's perfectly okay to cry," she said.

His tears soon dried up and he told her what had happened the week before, finding Choco sick that night at Turo, the Prophet telling him he was a channel, breaking into the Prophet's office. Nana listened intently, nodding and squeezing his hand when his voice shook.

"If we could only look at the drawing of the building again, show someone . . . But Leslie won't give it back. Dzifa and I think there's something's wrong somewhere. Maybe we're wrong. Maybe we're too young to understand the drawing."

"You know what you saw. Just because you're young does not make you wrong."

He snuggled back against the smooth brown leather of her car seat. His fear faded away as the miles between them and the House of Fire increased. By the time the wavy palms of Tamarind Ridge appeared, a scene had been seared in his mind, one he knew he would never forget: Prophet Yakayaka's look of surprise, his loosening hold around Ato's head. Nana's voice booming through the Hall of Fire. She had struck an unexpected blow: she had struck Prophet Yakayaka like a cassowary.

Much later that evening, after supper, Ato sat with Nana on the front porch. She had set two hot mugs of cocoa on the table for them with a slice each of warm banana cake. Nana rubbed her hand tenderly down his arm. His head rested against her shoulder.

"Ato, seeing you lying on this sofa reminds me of a big birthday party I threw here years ago. I enjoyed watching you wolfing food down and running around. I showed you off to all my friends. While the adults danced, you bounced around too, until you were so exhausted you collapsed on this sofa and fell asleep."

Only then did he realize where he was sitting: on the sofa. And suddenly it felt like the safest place to be.

"I remember that party so well, Nana," he smiled. It was time, he thought, to ask that question that had lurked in his mind for a long time. "Nana, why did Mum and I stop coming here?"

Her smile turned wistful. "My belief, Ato, is that the sight of you lying here, spread-eagled, dead to the party music . . . made your mother afraid. She had her reason. But I think someone has taken advantage of that fear."

"What was her reason, Nana?"

And again, Nana's eyes looked through and past him, into a world he had not been a part of. She didn't answer. He snuggled deeper into the lumpy comfort of the sofa, resting in comfy silence, sipping his cocoa. How different this evening felt from the frightful afternoon he'd had.

"Nana?

She touched his hand.

"Are you mad at Mum?"

Nana looked toward the garden. "Am I mad at your mother?" She pointed to the towering silhouettes in her garden, lit up by the crescent moon. "Look. Those trees all grew from one small seed. We admire the trees and enjoy their fruit. But we forget to admire the life force in the tiny seed they grow from."

What is she talking about? he wondered.

She caressed the creeper with purple flowers growing along the wooden lattice that framed the porch. "Children have a life force. Adults want to train children to grow gently, in the right direction. All we need to do is guide and lead that life force in you. That's harder than it sounds. We get confused. And like all of us, your mum too gets worried about which direction is right. So she turns to the Prophet for advice." Nana set her mug down and faced him, cross-legged. "Ato, you cannot blame the chicken for keeping close to the ground. It scratches there for grain and ants and flies.

It doesn't have to fly high. So it sees no reason why anything else should try to. High up is a place of fear for the chicken. And yet for the falcon, high up is where it finds freedom to live true to itself. As the saying goes, the falcon does not hunt flies. So to answer you, Ato: No. I'm not mad at your mum. Because I too was once like her."

"No way!"

But Nana was serious. "I too had a child who was flying into terrain I knew nothing about. After we go to the Zongo tomorrow, you'll understand."

◆ ◆ ◆ ◆ ◆

The next day, late morning, Ato followed Nana out her gate, down the quiet street and through the grassy field where laughing children tossed balls and sticks about. At the crumbling bank of the stream, he inhaled short breaths so the rotten air wouldn't fill his lungs. Nana started down the crumbling bank first. He picked his way behind her down the muddy path and onto a wooden plank that formed a bridge across the stream. It rattled as they stepped on it. Beneath him, plastic bottles and polythene bags floated downstream in the brown water. Weeds, reeds and slime-covered stones poked out of the stream. Bare-chested children waded in knee deep, playing with nets and colored plastic pails. On the other side of the stream, a pile of garbage made up of plastic bottles, shredded shopping bags, and cassava and plantain peelings greeted them. He wrinkled his nose.

"This is one of the better days," Nana said, amused. "I told you about the toilet situation here."

In the Zongo, buildings huddled close to each other, divided by narrow, uneven paths. Nana stepped quickly and lightly on the rough terrain—as if she knew it well. Ato had to keep his eyes on the path, hopping over stones that jutted out of the ground like bad teeth. On either side were single-room homes with small, net-covered windows. In many places the netting hung in limp shreds. Thin curtains sagged from string stretched across the windows. As they walked further from the stream, the stench thinned out and gave way to a warm, yeasty smell. He recognized the aroma of fermenting grain soaking in water before being milled.

He was beginning to pant. Nana didn't break her pace, hopping along the dusty path as it zigzagged between the little homes. Old women with chewing sticks poking out from between their lips and swathed in sweeping rainbow-colored scarves sat on plastic chairs by the open doors of their rooms. They waved cheerily at Nana, calling out greetings in a language he did not understand. Nana answered them just as cheerfully, waving back as she trotted on. After a couple of minutes, they hit a narrow, tarred street. It was crowded with yellow-and-white taxis, rusty minibuses, goats, chickens, dogs, and people—lots of people. Shops lined the road on both sides, with small glass fronts that allowed a view of shoes, clothes, perfumes and lotions for sale.

There was no pavement. Pedestrians hurried in different directions alongside the traffic, bumping into each other without apology. Ato puffed along behind Nana, narrowly avoiding a chicken with her brood of six or seven chicks. It swung a peck in the direction of his feet and clucked its irritation. They skirted a pile of sand and a stack of cement blocks where perspiring workmen shoveled sand and cement into a concrete mixer right alongside the street. He jumped when a taxi honked behind him. The driver glanced hopefully at them, indicating with a thumb that he was available for hire. Nana shook her head. Street hawkers with boiled groundnuts artfully stacked in flat pans balanced on their heads strolled past, calling out their wares. And along the entire length of the choked road, peddlers sat fanning themselves behind rough wooden tables piled high with bananas, oranges and basins of millet, rice, corn, beans and groundnuts.

"Don't knock over anyone's wares or we'll have to pay for them," Nana warned.

Suddenly she stopped in front of a doorway. It led into a sheltered space with tables covered in green oilcloth and chairs arranged around them. People sat eating with their fingers from large bowls. The aroma of waakye and fried plantain hit his nostrils and reminded him he hadn't had lunch. A lanky man with a trim black beard and a curved nose stepped out through an open archway at the far end. His eyes lit up in unmasked joy when they met Nana's, and he spread out his arms.

"Mama!" he exclaimed, giving her a bear hug. "Akwaaba!" He

stepped back and looked at Ato with eager, welcoming eyes. Nana smiled and nodded.

The man clapped his hands on Ato's shoulders and looked down at him with warm chocolate eyes. "You are my brother's son! You look just like your father, too." He hugged him, stepped back and playfully punched his shoulder. "I have longed to see you! My name is Yusuf."

CHAPTER EIGHTEEN

◊ ◊ ◊ ◊ ◊ ◊ ◊ ◊ ◊

"Yusuf! The same Yusuf Nana told me about?"

Yusuf broke into another smile. "De only Yusuf." He touched his forefingers together. "Your daddy was my best buddy. We were like this. Tight."

"My daddy? Did you know him?" He glanced at Nana in confusion.

Nana nodded and smiled as Yusuf ushered them to a table and sat them down. Ato's chair rocked slightly on the uneven stone floor. Why hadn't Nana mentioned that Yusuf had been his father's friend? Had BB been his father's friend too? He digested the surprising news as he looked around. It was a chop bar, clearly a popular eating spot, serving food to people who trooped in from the busy street outside. A team of attendants on the right wearing blue hair nets and white aprons served a long takeout line. Yusuf signaled to a young man wearing a blue T-shirt with *Fauzia's Kitchen* written in cursive across it. The man disappeared and reappeared with a tray bearing bottled water and three glasses.

"Welcome back, Ma," the waiter smiled to Nana.

"Thank you, Francis," Nana smiled back. She poured herself a chilled glass of water.

Yusuf took a seat at their round table. He barked out an instruction to another young waiter, who scurried up with two glasses of a frothy brown drink.

"Fula," Yusuf explained to Ato. "From millet and sugar and spice."

Ato took a cautious sip from the glass. It was creamy and spicy. He took a bigger mouthful. "I like fula!"

"Your daddy, my BB—he liked it a lot."

Ato was reaching for his drink. His hand froze. BB. The bustle in the restaurant around him faded as light flooded his mind.

"So, Nana, what you told me was—?"

"—was about your father—my son."

Click. Click. Connect. Ato gasped. "And that horrid woman, your neighbor . . . that was you, Nana?"

"That was me, indeed, Ato."

Just then a large older woman with a colorful head wrap emerged from the kitchen behind the servers. Her round face split into a grin when she saw Nana.

"Serwa!" she exclaimed.

"Fauzia!" Nana beamed as they embraced each other.

"My grandson, Ato," Nana said proudly. Fauzia clasped him against the folds of her ample spice-scented robe, rocking him, and exclaiming loudly in Hausa.

Fauzia was his mother, Yusuf said to Ato, after she had released him. Together they run this street restaurant. After a short, hearty conversation, she waddled back into the kitchen.

Ato's attention snapped back. "Nana, I can't believe it! BB in your story was my dad!"

Nana and Yusuf laughed.

Yusuf's eyes crinkled up with laughter. "Everyone called him Ekow. But I called him BB: he was my Best Buddy. I played with your dad everywhere, near de stream, in your nana's house." He smacked his lips. "I ate fine food from Nana here. I never tasted sandwiches like Nana's before—mmm—tuna, chicken, corned beef!"

He winked at Nana.

"You like de food I bring you from here?" Yusuf asked him. "All my BB's favorite foods."

"I love it!" Ato grinned.

Ato wanted to hear everything from Yusuf, but the man himself had a lot to ask Ato. It was obvious he had heard a lot about him, even asking about Dzifa, Leslie, Nnoma and their natural pesticide project. "You will go to Nnoma, Ato," he said with a firm nod. "Your daddy always said you would go there. There was something there he said he would show you when you were older. You will go."

Ato wished he could share his confidence.

He and Nana had both placed their lunch orders. It would be served in two minutes, Yusuf promised.

"Your daddy, he was like a brother." He sighed, rubbing his hand thoughtfully along his pants-clad thigh. "When I was a boy, I stood on my side of de water and I watched your daddy and his friends. We watched each other de way a snake and a mongoose would watch each other. They feared us. We feared their parents. Many mornings, my friends and I here in the Zongo did not go to school. We pushed carts, carrying t'ings for people—kenkey and waakye to de roadside for de sellers. We fetched water in plastic cans and metal buckets from de local water dealer and sold de water to homes for money. Here, at de time, many homes had no taps, no water. Anything else that needed to be moved, we moved. For coins."

"Didn't your parents want you to go to school?" Ato asked. Two plates of fried plantain with bean stew had been set before him and Nana. A bowl of water with a slice of lemon floating in it was also gently set on the table. He washed his hands in the bowl, picked up his fork and attacked his lunch.

"They did. But on de days we did not go to school we brought money home, so our mamas looked de other way," he said with a wink. "Sometimes your daddy and his friends, and me and my friends, we would meet at de mango tree near de stream and fight. At first they thought because we were small they could beat us." He flexed a powerful bicep and tapped it, chuckling softly. "We were slim but we had power. We always beat them. They were their mama's babies. They ate with forks and knives. Like you. We ate with these." He rubbed his fingers together. "But de teacher, Mr.

Bempong, he called us for English classes. And he gave us cookies and orange juice. And soon your daddy and I, we became best friends. I taught him how to climb a tree like a monkey. He crossed the stream to my side, and I taught him to push a water-cart. He brought his toys to the field, and we played with them together."

"Like the water pistol?" Ato grinned.

He smiled. "Aah, that water pistol! I'd never seen one like that before! It could shoot a fat lizard from de tree. We enjoyed that water pistol very much. I showed him my sleeping mat on de floor of my room. He took me to his big house when your nana had gone out. He let me sit on his bed. I'd never seen such a soft bed. And de wood floor of de house . . . smooth, like glass! We wore your daddy's socks and had slide races on de floor. We ate together too. I gave him my mama's food. He gave me his mama's food. Then one day, we were sitting on de porch sofa eating . . ." He glanced cheekily at Nana.

Nana rolled her eyes. "I was so mad! All I could see was that boy with dirty feet on my precious sofa."

Ato winced. It was hard to imagine Nana being so horrid.

"And he was eating my son's food! And playing with an expensive water pistol I had bought him. Ekow had begged for it for months and I got it for his tenth birthday. I ran up the steps, snatched the water pistol and shooed Yusuf away. Afterward I scolded Ekow. I wanted him to stop playing with Zongo boys and get good grades in school and make me proud so my friends could see what a fine gentleman he was."

"Just like Mum!" Ato groaned.

She nodded. "Exactly like your mother."

"And that was when you had a row with the mums across the stream?"

"Yes," Yusuf said. "And after de mamas had de big quarrel at de stream, everything changed." He pressed a hairy hand to his chest. "I was angry. I was hurting here. I missed de games we played. I missed de food. But I missed my BB de most. I thought he had told your nana here things about me, that I was a thief. He tried to come back to de stream. But me and my friends didn't trust him anymore. We chased him away. Later, I saw him playing with other boys and I thought he had forgotten me. I was angry. I wanted to show him. So one day we cornered him at de mango tree, and I ran away with de water pistol." A rueful expression shadowed his face. "I played with it, but it was not de same as playing with my BB. Then, foolish me, I took it back for de Saturday classes with de good teacher. You know about that?"

Ato nodded, his fork suspended in the air with a chunk of plantain at the end of it.

"I tried to run away." Yusuf shook his head in wry amusement. "Mr. Bempong caught me. Marched me to Mam's house. Everyone in Tamarind Ridge was behind me, calling me a thief. My BB was walking behind us. Your nana, she was sitting on de porch sofa when we got there. They asked her about de water pistol and she said yes, that was Ekow's water pistol."

Nana spoke. "I asked him: Ekow, isn't this your water pistol? Did that rascal boy take it from you?"

Yusuf looked down. When he looked up, his eyes were wet.

"Your daddy looked at me, then he looked at your nana and all de people around, and then he looked back at me an' he said: "Yusuf didn't take it, Mama. I gave it to him a long time ago. It's his now, not mine.""

There was silence around the table.

"So I walked back to de garage class . . . with my water pistol," Yusuf said.

Nana turned to Ato. "Your dad stood up for his friend in front of all those kids and the angry mothers, and what did I do? After they had all left my home, I yelled at him for giving away the water pistol. I told him he would never have another toy again if he was going to give them away to a Zongo boy."

Yusuf scratched his close-cropped head. "My best buddy did not want that fence to be built. It never was. Even now, years later, kids from both sides of de stream meet and play together on that field.

"Your daddy and I grew up. He went to boarding school and university and we were best friends. He was designing sites, nature sites and things like that. Then he got married. I traveled to another city, and never met your mama. But I still saw my BB sometimes. Then one day my cousin told me about a new bird island. They were trying to build on one side of it, and it was very difficult. It was a mountain with big rocks. My cousin said it was a hard job, too hard for anyone. I told my cousin that I knew someone who could crack de hard mountain."

"You see"—Nana reached for Ato's hand—"your father first heard about Nnoma from Yusuf."

Yusuf interlocked his fingers beneath his chin. "One evening BB came to my place. I had not seen him for some time because he was working at Nnoma. He looked tired that day, but we sat here and he told me about you, you had started walking!

"We talked, we laughed and we ate my mama's waakye. Then he was going back an' I walked with him. It was very dark, before de new moon come up. Normally I would say goodbye at de mango tree. When we got there, I reminded him of de water pistol. Normally he would laugh, but this time . . ." Yusuf shook his head.

"I knew something wrong because he always laughed a lot, my BB. He told me I could go back home, but I did not like the way he looked, so I crossed the field with him. Then he started to cough. He could not stand. He stopped talking.

"It was dark, with nobody around, so I picked him up from de ground like a baby. I carried him and ran to your nana's house. I banged on de gate. She opened it. We put him on de porch sofa.

"Nana called de ambulance and hospital and was trying to wake him. I ran to call a doctor from down de road. I came with de doctor, but when we got there, before de ambulance arrived, my BB was gone. Right there on de sofa."

A lump formed in Ato's throat, even as his brain began to make sense of the thoughts flooding in. His father had died on the sofa. So that was it.

It started here, and . . . That was the sentence Nana had left unfinished that first night.

I'm scared. Was that why the sofa frightened his mother? Because his father had died on it?

History repeats itself. Was that what the Prophet had meant? That he too would die on the couch?

Nana spoke first. "Your father had a rare heart condition. At first your mother accepted it. We helped and comforted each other. But some years later she began to believe I had tried to revive your father myself, with some homemade herbal potion, that I must have kept him too long from getting to the hospital. And she began to stay away from me, and stopped visiting me."

Yusuf shook his head. "I never ran so fast in my life when I was going to get de doctor. We did everything we could."

Yusuf rose abruptly and disappeared from view through an archway at the back that led away from the eating area.

Nana kept her hand over his. "Ato, your mother misses your father. We all do. She is sad. And afraid for you. Like I used to be. Your father was a normal boy. Like you. But I never saw that. I wanted him to be perfect. I was so afraid of him crossing the stream and playing with Yusuf that my fear took over me. You're a lot like your father was when he was your age, Ato. But your mother can't see that; she's searching so hard to see the man in you that, like I did, she doesn't see the brave, smart, loyal boy she has."

Yusuf walked back to them and sat down. In his hand was a crumpled brown paper bag. "Your daddy—he was a friend, in good times and bad times. I never felt afraid when he was with me.

De day everyone called me thief, my BB stayed close by me. And on that last day . . ." He took a deep breath and then continued, "I was happy I stayed close to my BB. I was happy I did not leave him alone."

He pulled his hand out of the bag and withdrew an old blue and green plastic water pistol. He smiled. "It still works. It still has five different shooting sounds and flashing colors."

CHAPTER NINETEEN

◊ ◊ ◊ ◊ ◊ ◊ ◊ ◊ ◊

THE RIDE BACK HOME FROM NANA'S ON SUNDAY AFTERNOON had been a nerve-racking one. What would his mother do to him, after he'd walked away from her in front of everyone at the House of Fire? Did she plan to drag him back to the House of Fire as soon as Nana's car disappeared? He bit his inner lip when his mother met them at the gate.

"Go on ahead, Ato," Nana said to him. He obeyed, walking indoors. Standing hidden behind the curtain, he watched Nana and Mum have a long conversation outside. Eventually, Nana drove off. His mother walked back in and shut the front door. He looked at her warily.

"Did you have a good weekend?" she asked.

"Yes, Mum," he answered hesitantly.

"I'm not going to say anything about last Friday, Ato." She spoke softly. "I think it would have helped, but Nana thinks differently. I hope she's right."

She offered him a glass of fresh pineapple juice and asked him to do his homework while she sat close by watching video clips on her phone.

She began to believe I had tried to revive him myself . . . that I must have kept him too long . . .

We did everything we could.

Your mother misses your father. We all do.

Fragments from Saturday's conversation replayed in his head while he worked. He stole glances at his mother, sitting at the dining table with him, her head bent over her phone. He hoped one day he would make her proud of him and she would stop feeling sad and scared.

The next day was Monday. Classes always seemed to last longer than they did the rest of the week. Mercifully, by 3 p.m. school was out. His mother picked him up on time, and stayed on at home for her afternoon meeting at the House of Fire.

He scribbled out a few hurried lines for his Literature homework. At four o'clock he convinced his mother he was done and hurried out the front door, where he promptly tumbled over Philomena's outstretched legs. She sat slumped like a sack on her cleaning stool. Her duster had slipped to the floor. He noticed that over the last few Mondays she'd been as sluggish as a caterpillar about the house. Today was no different. She woke with a start, snatched up her duster and began attacking the porch rails.

"You should not be going to Turo," she chided. Her eyes were dull and bleary. "No one should go there."

He trotted off before she could say any more. He didn't want to hear anything about evil in Turo. It made him uncomfortable. Instead he thought about their radishes and spring onions and how they would have grown another inch or two. And he thought about how proud his mother would be when he won a place to Nnoma. Soon the rock that marked Turo was in sight. Leslie was already there. And Dzifa.

But why were they both just standing there, staring?

Thump-thump-thump. His heart leapt into his throat. What was it this time? He broke into a run. The sight in Turo hit him like a punch in his stomach.

He stared. He blinked. But the scene of horror did not disappear. Leslie and Dzifa stood dumb and motionless. Where were the bright, healthy green plants—their spinach, their okra, their lettuce, their radishes? What were these blackened and burnt lumps? He looked around wildly. There was no one across the pond. Falling to his knees, he plunged his hands into the soil, snatching at charred leaves and stems, trying to fish them out, prop them up. There had to be something left! They couldn't all be ruined!

"Don't just stand there!" he shouted tearfully to Dzifa and Leslie. "Maybe we can dig them up and save them. Get some water!"

But the plants he held crumbled to ashy shreds in his trembling hands. This was no accident. Someone had done this. He was sure he knew who.

"The Prophet did this," he said bitterly, staring at the ground.

"He did! I know he did!" Dzifa cried.

"You can't say that!" Leslie protested. "That's a false accusation."

Rage rose like boiling lava in Ato's chest. "He wants to pay me back for getting away! Our project was doing fine!"

Leslie glanced from side to side, as though some wild creature was about to pounce on him. "The Prophet is right, there's something wrong here. It's the evil he spoke about. We should have stopped coming here. We should have chosen another project," he whimpered.

Dzifa, like a magpie on attack, thrust her face into his. "Why didn't you choose another project?" she screeched. "Hmm, Leslie? What ideas did you have? All you could think of was cleaning your hands ten times a day!"

Ato felt the crushing weight of defeat. He sat heavily on the ground and shut his eyes. He was a falcon spinning helplessly down to earth from the sky. His wings had been hacked off.

◆ ◆ ◆ ◆ ◆

That evening after his mother had returned from her meeting, Ato bit his quivering lip and tearfully told her what had happened. For the second time in a few days, his tears brimmed over.

She inhaled sharply, in genuine shock, clapping her hand over her mouth. "I'm so sorry, Ato. You've all put so much into it." She hugged him close. "Never mind, maybe it's for the best."

Her words speared his heart and he pushed her away angrily. "How can it be for the best?!"

"Ato, Nnoma is very hard to get into. There was no guarantee you'd get in. It's not for everyone."

"I'm not just everyone. I'm Ato! And I wanted to go there! I worked so hard!"

"Lower your voice. I'm your mother."

But Ato was deafened by the roar of his pain. "You don't care, Mum! All you care about is for me to look good in front of everyone. I bet if my dad were here he would have helped me and he would have made sure nothing happened to my project, but you don't care! I bet you're happy now!"

"Go to your room at once!"

He stormed off, and for the first time since he was four years old, he slammed his door behind him so hard his bedroom windows rattled. Throwing himself on his bed, he buried his head under his pillow. Even then he heard her on the phone with Leslie's mother, clucking in agitation and agreeing that deliverance would have been helpful. He ground his teeth until his tongue bled. He wasn't offered dinner but he was not hungry and he didn't want to see his mother.

He shut his eyes and pressed his face against the sheet. He was a peregrine falcon, wingless and wounded, falling through the sky, chased by a flock of angry birds—parakeets, chickens, crows and magpies. Below him surged the waves of a stormy ocean. The birds cawed and snapped at his tail, ripping away his feathers. The wind lashing his face was agony. In the distance, he glimpsed the peak of Nnoma, wreathed in thick cloud. His powerful wings were gone—he could not make it.

He was plummeting down, down, down toward the churning depths. Just before he slammed into the waves, a long, bloody claw appeared in front of him. He steeled himself to be impaled, but it curled around him and he was snatched up, away from the ocean, and dropped tenderly, up on the rock. His ragged breathing slowed down, and he fell asleep.

♦ ♦ ♦ ♦ ♦

The next day he struggled to pay attention in class. It was Tuesday and that meant the first lesson was Biology. The pictures of green plants filled him with rage, pain and a sense of injustice. The Prophet had done this, he was certain. And the Prophet himself was hiding something. He would take the drawing and let everyone see what the Prophet was planning. Ato cornered Leslie after the lesson. If Leslie didn't give him the drawing, he threatened, he would tell everyone that Leslie had been part of the break-in. What would the Prophet think of him then?

Leslie looked anguished. "Ato, but we should never have—"

"Leslie, if you say what we shouldn't have done one more time, one of us will get hurt and it won't be me," Dzifa threatened.

Like a wounded parakeet, Leslie fluttered off to the library, took a seat directly in front of the librarian and stuck his face deep into a book, avoiding them both the rest of the day.

By Wednesday, Ato had decided on a different strategy. Leslie was right. It was a terrible thing to have taken the drawing, he told Leslie. It had to be returned at once. He would find a way to put it back—if Leslie gave it to him.

Leslie refused.

On Thursday morning, Ato sat hunched over on his bed for several minutes after he had woken up. He didn't want to see or talk to anyone. He just wanted to stay in his room and eat peanut butter sandwiches and sleep. His annoyed mother hustled him out to the car. He had to stop behaving as if someone had died, she scolded. There would always be another chance.

Would there be another chance? He wondered disconsolately to Dzifa during the break. Maybe he had taken the words of his father's letter too seriously. His father was dead, so what did he know? Their project would probably never have been good enough to go to Nnoma.

"I bet your dad wouldn't have given up so easily," Dzifa argued, following him to his mum's car after school. "Look at the mega-problems he had to handle when he was helping to build Nnoma. You can't just give up! Yeah, maybe we missed out on Nnoma this time, but Ato, we know there's something shady about Prophet Yak. We have to find out what it is!"

"Find out yourself," Ato muttered. He yanked open his mother's car door, slumped down and slammed the door shut in Dzifa's face.

On Friday morning he packed his bag to go to Nana's. After several minutes hunting fruitlessly for his sneakers he remembered: he'd left them in a bag in the cleaning cupboard the night Choco was sick. His mother was outside in her car waiting. He hurried out to the cleaning cupboard. It was cluttered, as usual, and he rummaged around for his shoes, grumbling to himself about Philomena. He picked up a black shopping bag and opened it. It contained a bundled-up dress of Philomena's, black with pink flowers. It smelled of smoke. And there was something else. He looked at the dress for a moment. His harried mind flashed signals that he could not make sense of.

Parp!

He jumped at the sharp honk from his mum's car. He shoved aside a large yellow plastic container. Finally—the shopping bag he was looking for was behind it. A thick, greenish-blue liquid spilled from the container. He wrinkled his nose at the sickly sweet, acidic smell, grabbed the shopping bag with his shoes in it, and thrust it into his overnight bag.

After school was out, on the drive to Nana's with his mother, he sat quietly while she talked about the exceptional person his father had been. Ato was not listening. He was a peregrine falcon with new, strong wings, perched high on a crag. Below him, thick storm clouds had blocked the view he had of his target, Nnoma. Suddenly a light flashed on in his head. Then a hole appeared through the heavy cloud. His target was still not in view. But something else had appeared: his prey. His powerful heart began to pound, supplying oxygen to his wings and brain: oxygen he would need for the hunt.

CHAPTER TWENTY

◊ ◊ ◊ ◊ ◊ ◊ ◊ ◊ ◊

"NANA, I CAN'T BELIEVE I DIDN'T SPOT THAT CLUE WHEN I saw her dress in the bag this morning. It hit me on the way here! Mum was honking this morning and I was trying to get to the car quickly so I didn't figure it out then: those spikes grow in only one place—in Turo!"

Ato was sitting on the arm of the porch sofa, leaning against Nana. "And they were all over Philomena's dress . . . hidden in the cleaning cupboard. She said she doesn't go there, but she must have, to have had so many spikes in her dress. And her dress smelled of smoke, and there was that blue-green liquid stuff! Nana, that's the liquid we saw in the Prophet's office!"

It was difficult to sit still with the frantic activity going on in his head. He began to pace the porch, up and down beneath the swinging porch light.

"Nana, the night Choco was sick, someone else was there at Turo apart from the Prophet. Maybe it was Philomena! Does Philomena know something about how our project burned up? Does she know anything about why things are dying there?" He groaned and collapsed beside her. "How do I find out? I bet my dad would know what to do. And I bet he wouldn't be afraid either!"

Nana rubbed his shoulder. "Your father was afraid so many times, Ato. But he learned not to let his fear stop him. That day when I asked your father in front of everyone about the water pistol, his lips were trembling. He was afraid. But he still defended Yusuf. Years later he told me that he knew if he claimed the pistol, that would be it: the fence would go up. So he risked my anger to save his friend and keep the field open. He did it afraid."

"Nana, somebody stole my chance of going to Nnoma. And it's not just about me. It's about Papa Kojo too. You should've seen his face. He's so worried. He's grown his vegetables for years. Now someone has ruined that for him; that's how he makes a living. And Choco . . ." His voice cracked. "What do I do?"

"You can do something. Or you can do nothing. What would make you feel better?"

He sat bolt upright. "I have to find out what's going on! Something inside me tells me I have to do something. But is that me? Or is some spirit trying to get me into trouble again?"

Nana hugged him to her. The sweet tang of citronella from the candles along the porch wafted in their direction.

"Ato, we all have spirits inside. Noisy spirits that shout— You're not good enough, You'll never make it, You're worthless. Quietly tell them: Go Away.

"Say it often enough, and their voices will fade away. That's when you get to hear the quieter spirits telling you—Try harder. Love him. Forgive her. It's not over."

Nana caressed his shoulder. "You know, Ato, the director of Nnoma had planned the fifth phase of Nnoma, the Dawn Locus, to be the final and most spectacular phase. It faced east. People approaching the island from miles away would see the sunrays explode from it, flooding the landscape with brilliant light. It would be the iconic image of the island.

"The plan was to remold the rock and construct a path for walkers. Steps would be cut into steep rock, below the point where falcons roosted above. But it was treacherous rock. There had been an earth tremor there years earlier, and the rock had slid and shifted. Some minds wanted to give it up. It could not be done, they said.

"There was another side of the mountain, facing southwest. It would not face the rising sun, but it would be easier to build the walkway, and the climb would be easy. But the director did not want an easy climb. He had never intended the Dawn Locus to be for the fainthearted. He kept his vision. It could be done, he said. All it needed was the right person.

"Now, as Yusuf said, he had a cousin who was working at Nnoma. That cousin mentioned the director's vision to Yusuf. Yusuf told your father. It could be done, your father said. And your father put a team of experts together. He believed in working with people—Better together, he always said. They thought up their plan. Then they attended an interview at Nnoma and presented their plan. People said he was wrong, it could not be done. He was too young; he did not know how difficult it was.

"Just because you're young does not mean you are wrong, the director said to your father. And guess what, Ato?"

"It was done," Ato whispered.

"Yes. Ekow died a few months after it was finished. Now, every few years, a few special people from around the world are invited to challenge themselves to the Dawn Locus. There is a plaque in your father's name carved into the rock. I never saw his strength, and courage, when he was a boy like you."

"You changed, Nana."

"Ato, when the rhythm of the drum changes, the dancers must also change their steps. I badly wanted your father to be a man whom everyone would admire and who would make me proud. I thought crossing the stream and making friends with kids like Yusuf would ruin my dreams for him. But crossing that stream was the best thing your father did. All that time spent outdoors with Yusuf built something special in him—a brave spirit. He was never one to give up. And he passed that spirit on to you."

Ato digested her words, and relaxed beside her with her arm resting lightly on him. The citronella candles glowed softly in their stands. The flames flickering in the evening breeze reminded him of something else: his burning desire to get to the bottom of what happened at Turo. It wasn't only about Nnoma now. It was about being brave and doing what he thought was the right thing.

"The bird that pecks at a rock, trusts in the strength of its beak. Whatever you decide, Ato, be sensible. And remember, I will always be on your side."

How did she know what he was thinking? He was lying where his dad had been born, and where he had whispered his last goodbye to Nana and Yusuf. Could it be that his dad's spirit could hear his thoughts, and whisper them back to Nana?

He smiled. He liked that thought. He closed his eyes, but not to sleep. The falcon's instinct compelled him to move. He had missed his target, but now he was hungry for the kill. He could stay sheltered here. Or he could risk the storm to catch his prey. It would take skill. But he was born for speed and for the hunt.

CHAPTER TWENTY-ONE

◊ ◊ ◊ ◊ ◊ ◊ ◊ ◊ ◊

ATO HAD NEVER FELT MORE ALERT ON A MONDAY MORNING. After his weekend at Nana's, his thoughts had gelled into one solid idea. Around him, dull-eyed kids dragged themselves back into the school assembly hall for the headmistress's address before the day's lessons. He'd caught Dzifa before assembly to bounce his thoughts off her: There was something very wrong with the drawing in Prophet Yak's office. But that was not the only thing odd. He'd been thinking about the second sheet too.

"The one with the money and dates?" Dzifa asked.

He nodded. "Remember its title?"

"Fund-raising for Agoro, or something like that."

"Something like that. But not quite. It said 'Fund-raising *by* Agoro.'"

"For and by. Those are two very different meanings," Dzifa said slowly. She blinked rapidly, the way she did in magpie mode. "Is he using Agoro to raise funds, or is he raising funds for Agoro?"

"It's time to visit Agoro, Dzifa."

Dzifa threw herself at him and locked her arms around him. "Yessss! Let's see what he's really up to!"

"Let go!" he gasped.

She released her lobster-claw hold, and he sagged against the wall of the school assembly hall, filling his lungs with air as she danced an excited magpie jig. The peal of the assembly bell drowned her delighted squealing. They joined the shuffle of students finding seats.

"Now we just need to get Leslie on board," Ato said.

The magpie squinted at him. "Okay. We may as well decide we're not going."

Ato grimaced. This was going to be tricky. They seated themselves behind a pillar that hid them from the view of the prefect on duty.

"Leslie will only end up getting us into more trouble," she whispered. "That's if he even wants to join us." Her tone hardened. "Look at how useful he was as a guard when we searched the House of Fire. We should've just plonked our scarecrow there to act as lookout."

"Leslie's not so bad," Ato protested stoutly. "He did give us warning at the House of Fire—we just didn't hear. And he took off with the drawing too. We just need to get it back from him. And listen, I checked out Agoro on Mum's laptop. It's a forty-five-minute drive away—without traffic. The taxi ride there and back will cost one month's pocket money—from both of us. But Leslie has money. And a phone to help us find Agoro." He remembered what Nana had said about his father. "We're better together, Dzifa."

"Get Leslie if you must. But don't blame me if he ends up ruining it."

Ato smiled. "Leave him to me, Dzifa."

Convincing Leslie required careful strategy. Lying was necessary, he thought regretfully. His chance at last to corner Leslie came that day after school, on their way to the parking lot where both their mothers were already waiting.

An old friend of his nana's had come to visit her that weekend while he was there, he told Leslie. She was loaded. Her handbag by some-designer-or-other bulged with cash. The old friend had taken them out to an expensive meal—where she'd casually tipped the waiters one hundred percent of their shockingly high bill. She'd tossed a hundred-cedi note to every street beggar they'd met on their way back.

Leslie pursed his lips piously. "I hope she earns her money honestly."

"Course she does," Ato assured him. "She's been saving since she was a child—just like you."

Leslie nodded approvingly.

Ato crossed his fingers and continued, hoping he wouldn't stumble over his well-rehearsed untruth. This old friend had heard about the Prophet and his good work at Agoro, he told Leslie. She'd seen a TV program where a charming young boy wearing his Sunday best stood beside the Prophet, talking about his goodness. Her heart had been touched. It was a wealthy heart. So she wanted to write a fat check for the children in Agoro. The only problem was she hadn't actually seen Agoro. She didn't know anyone who had, either. If someone she knew and trusted would go directly there and come back to tell her about the good work going on in Agoro, she would write a six-figure check. And she would add a note telling the Prophet that her gift was coming because of the endearing way that boy standing beside him had spoken.

Leslie grabbed Ato by the front of his shirt. "We must find a way to go there, and even take pictures for her! And tell her my name!"

"I gave her all your names," Ato assured him, smoothing down his shirt. "Plus your birthday. And your address."

Leslie high-fived Ato. "This is your best idea ever, Ato!" he chirped. "Not like those dangerous ones you and Dzifa thought of! You see, people want to give money to Agoro—because of me! And when we bring her pictures, everyone will see how kind Prophet Yakayaka is, giving the children good food and clothes and looking after them."

Ato nodded his approval of these noble deeds until his neck ached with guilt.

"My mother could drive us to Agoro."

"NO!" Ato grabbed Leslie's arm. By now they were within a few feet of their mothers.

"What?" Leslie turned a puzzled gaze at him.

"Don't tell anyone about our plan. This rich lady likes to do her good deeds in secret. She said the Bible says not to tell your left hand anything your right hand does. Your mum will tell someone, Leslie. You know she will. Then the old lady will get to hear somehow. And that will be the end of the money for Agoro. She'll give it to somebody else."

"I guess my mum isn't great with secrets," he said slowly, hesitantly.

♦ ♦ ♦ ♦ ♦

The next day, they discussed their plan before class. Or rather Ato discussed the plan with Leslie. Dzifa stood by looking pointedly in the opposite direction. Wednesday after school would be the best time to go. Both their mothers had activities that kept them busy till 6 p.m. If they left home at 4 p.m., they would be back home by 6 p.m.

"We won't need more than ten minutes there. Just so I can show my nana's rich friend what an amazing place it is. And by the way, Leslie," Ato added lightly, "we'll need, erm . . . money to get there. From you."

Leslie's shoulders sagged.

The following day, despite Leslie's reluctance to dip into any part of his nest egg, Ato successfully steered him along the weedy back lanes of their neighborhood to the main road. Dzifa trailed them by a couple of paces. The itchy detour was to avoid the unnecessary setback of bumping into parents or neighbors.

The pavement along the main road was cluttered with rows of kiosks offering gaudy clothes, packaged food and mobile phones for sale. They wove behind them, skirting the rear ends of broad-backed women roasting ripe plantain on coals and frying yam slices in cauldrons of bubbling oil. Their ducking and weaving brought them to the ATM outside the bank.

"I was saving for a good reason." Leslie's voice was high-pitched.

"It doesn't get better than this," Ato assured him.

"I don't know if this is a good reason if I can't tell my mother about it."

"Mothers don't understand. They peck ants on the ground when you have to fly."

"What?" The parakeet turned a pair of bewildered eyes at Ato.

"Never mind," Ato said, helping Leslie polish the ATM touch pads with hand sanitizer. It sounded better when Nana said it. "You'll be the hero. The Prophet will love you even more. Your mum will be so proud of you. You'll be on TV again and the whole nation will find out how much money you brought in for Agoro."

An impatient and growing line of people had formed behind them when Leslie finally withdrew 160 cedis from his savings account. He'd get most of it back, Ato comforted him, feeling guilt pile like bricks on his head. Together with the 40 cedis he and Dzifa had between them, they now had 200 cedis. It wouldn't cost more than 100 cedis for a return journey. Leslie would have 100 cedis left.

"And I'll give all of that 100 cedis to Prophet Yakayaka for Agoro," Leslie said, comforted.

At the taxi stand a few yards from the bank, they were waved into the first of a straggly line of yellow-and-white taxis alongside a crooked wooden post that read TAXIS.

"Pooh." Dzifa had strapped herself into the front seat of the lopsided car. She turned to the taxi driver. "What have you been carrying? Fish?"

He slid her an unfriendly look.

"Take us to Agoro, please," Ato said from the backseat.

The driver frowned. "Where is that?"

Ato shot a you-see-why-we-need-Leslie look at Dzifa. With the help of Leslie's phone they were soon on their way. Arrival would be in forty-eight minutes, the map announced. Thanks to Leslie's hesitation at the ATM, it was already 4:15 p.m.

"Eighty cedis to Agoro," the driver muttered. He ignored their howls of protest. It was a long way away and that area had a terrible road, he said flatly, bumping his way to the exit road with a speed that felt cruel for such a deformed taxi.

Ten minutes into their journey, Leslie's phone rang. Leslie glanced at his phone and clamped his fist over his mouth.

"My mother. I told her I'd be at your house, Ato."

"Don't answer," Ato warned. "We'll be back home in no time."

"But—"

Dzifa reached around, snatched the phone and tapped at the screen. She handed it back. "I blocked all calls."

"This is trouble. This is deception," the parakeet squeaked fretfully. "My mum will never trust me again. She just sent a message. She wants to know why I withdrew money."

Ato gritted his teeth. "We're on a mission, Leslie. Let's not ruin it. We'll be back by six."

"Will we? What if—"

Dzifa looked over her car seat. "Leslie, do you have an 'off' switch or do we just take your batteries out?"

The taxi driver squinted unpleasantly at them. "Do your parents know you're out here?"

"We're not paying you to ask questions," Dzifa said.

"Heh!" The taxi driver cleared his throat and spat a thick white gob out his window.

Leslie winced.

"Kids of today. No respect. If I were your father—"

"You're not my father."

"One more rude word and I'm gonna throw you out of my car," the driver growled to Dzifa. His car rattled at high speed over a ramp.

"Where's the law that says we can't be in a taxi by ourselves?"

The driver muttered something about bad parenting and directed his disgust to his gas pedal. For twenty-five minutes, the rickety taxi jounced in and out of potholes like a flying sardine tin. Just as Ato began to feel an ache in his behind, a wooden sign appeared. AGORO, it announced.

The driver turned off the main road onto a narrow, laterite track. The tall grass alongside it was blanketed in red dust. For mile after mile, the groaning taxi suffered across mounds and dips on the dirt road. No car approached from the opposite direction.

Finally, a long stretch of pristine white wall rose up, against the dusty grassland. It appeared to cover a sizable square area. As they clattered closer, a pair of towering black gates set below a high archway came into view. The letters A G O R O were painted in bright, welcoming colors along the curve of the arch. Beside the closed metal gate was a poky-looking security post. Its single window overlooked the street. Two thick men were visible through the glass. They were not going to be able to have a quick peek into Agoro by hanging about in front, Ato realized.

"Stop here," he ordered, behind a cluster of scrubby trees. They were within fifty yards of the gates. The taxi grated to a stop along the dirt road, and they clambered out.

Ato counted out the fare grandly and handed it over to the driver. "We'll be back in ten minutes," he said, patting the door with authority.

"What do I care?" The driver had switched his engine back on.

"But you have to wait for us," Ato protested.

"Why? You paid me to bring you here. It'll be one hundred cedis to take you back."

"One hundred cedis?" all three of them screeched in united horror.

"You saw how bad the road was."

"It's not the road that's bad, it's your driving," Dzifa scolded.

Ato looked up and down the road. There wasn't a car in sight. Nothing but tall, wavy grass, dry trees and a few cottages scattered so far apart it would take an hour to walk from one to the other.

The driver shifted into reverse gear.

"Seventy cedis," Ato said.

"Ninety. There'll be traffic going back." He backed his car onto the road.

"Eighty cedis," Ato pleaded. "That's all we have.

The magpie was hopping in indignation. "If you don't take us, we'll walk back and you'll drive all the way back with no fare. What kind of business sense is that, huh?"

The parakeet was whimpering by now. "I'll only have thirty cedis left."

The driver stopped. "So you have more money."

The magpie trod on the parakeet's foot.

"Ow!"

"Ninety cedis. Last price. Or I go." He turned his car around to face the direction they had come from.

"You can't leave us here. That's irresponsible! If anything happens to us, the police will come after you: you were the last person to see us!"

Ato stepped in front of Dzifa. "Okay, ninety cedis."

The driver switched off his engine at once.

Ato sighed in relief. "Can you stay behind this bush, out of sight? We'll be back in ten minutes." He tucked their return fare safely into his shorts.

Dzifa grumbled about the taxi driver as they crept along the bushes toward the long wall. The falcon fixed his eyes on his prey, Ato thought. When the prey moved, so did he. He kept adjusting his position in the air. His superior instinct could tell him where his prey would be next.

And by the time the prey got to that point, he would be there.

CHAPTER TWENTY-TWO

◊ ◊ ◊ ◊ ◊ ◊ ◊ ◊ ◊

ATO TOOK THE LEAD, SCURRYING THROUGH DENSE GRASS and the wild plants that grew against the freshly painted wall. The wall itself was a formidable construction of solid concrete that rose ten feet high and stretched down nearly the length of a soccer field.

"Why it so hard to get in?" Dzifa mused aloud.

The only openings were narrow rectangular holes along the bottom, spaced apart to let out rainwater. Leslie stood guard while Ato and Dzifa lay flat on their stomachs, peering through a hole each. On the other side of the wall sprawled a vast yard with vegetation that needed severe trimming. Ato's peephole allowed him a view of a U-shaped building. It looked like it was made up of several single rooms side by side. A row of taps were fixed to the wall outside the building. The concrete ground around the taps was pitted. Green mold fanned out around it.

"Hey." Two eyes appeared on the other side of Ato's hole. Ato jerked his head back but kept eye contact.

"You lookin' for somethin'?" a boy's voice said.

Ato glanced at Dzifa and Leslie. "Umm . . . we . . ."

"We heard about this place. From people. Good things," Dzifa said. "And we wanted to see it."

"So you believe everythin' people is telling you?"

"Who that?" A third eye joined Two Eyes behind Ato's hole.

"Yes, yes." Leslie bent over to see the owners of the disembodied voices. "We know this is a good place, and you get a lot of good food and—"

"We get gari an' beans mornin'," Two Eyes said. "Rice an' beans afternoon."

"Gari an' sugar, evening," Third Eye said.

"I know you eat better than that!" Leslie declared.

"Beans wiv stones," said Two Eyes.

"Rice wiv weevils," Third Eye added.

Ato and Dzifa exchanged looks.

"That's not true. If it's that bad, why don't you leave?" Leslie challenged.

Two Eyes dug a finger into his nostril. "Same why you couldna come in. And anyways we got nowhere to go. Things not good where we come from. So we jes stay here."

"Well, at least sometimes you get to eat butter bread and hot chocolate and beef stew and jollof rice with chicken, don't you? Sometimes?" Leslie had pressed his face close to the hole.

The eyes behind the peephole seemed to be enjoying their visitors. They had never had any of the tasty foods Leslie described, they swore. Every week trucks came to deliver the same moldy rice and gari and beans.

Leslie looked perplexed by this information. He stood in the sun, holding his phone, hands hanging limply at his sides.

Ato's struggled to calm his thoughts. The Prophet said he was feeding the kids with good food. These boys said he wasn't. Somebody was lying: who? There was one way to find out.

"Hey, can you take pictures for us?" Ato asked Two Eyes.

"Pictures? Of what?" Two Eyes sounded doubtful. "How?"

"Pictures of inside, what Agoro looks like. With this." Ato snatched Leslie's phone and thrust it through the hole.

"Hey!" Leslie plunged his hand through the hole. Too late. The phone was on the other side. He withdrew his bleeding knuckle. "Give it back!"

"Shushh!" Ato elbowed him.

"His hands aren't even clean, he stuck his finger in his nose!" Leslie screeched.

The eyes had disappeared. "Fine phone," they heard from behind the wall. The voice was thick with admiration.

"Take pictures—many—everywhere!" Dzifa urged.

Two Eyes reappeared. "Fine fine phone. How much you will give me for fine fine pictures?"

"Gimme my phone!"

Third Eye appeared. "Who this crying baby? Your broda?"

"Nope. Some guy we brought here for his money and his phone," Dzifa said smoothly.

"Okay. How much for fine pictures?"

"Does it always have to be about money?" Leslie mumbled mournfully.

"Five cedis," Ato said.

"Rich boy like you. With fine phone. Gimme ten cedis. I take fine photos for you."

"What?" Leslie's shriek pierced the air.

Ato clapped a hand over Leslie's mouth. "Ten cedis," he said, and shoved a note through the hole.

"Okay, rich boy. Wait for me."

All three eyes disappeared.

Leslie groaned and slumped to the ground against the wall. "Ato, are you crazy? What if he doesn't come back?"

"He will," Ato said confidently, settling on the grass.

Leslie stared at the twenty cedis he had left as if it were all he had to live on the rest of his life. Dzifa explored an ant nest nearby. Ato sat in the shade of the wall and wondered what the pictures would show them about Agoro.

But twenty long minutes later Ato wasn't so sure about the phone coming back. He was sweaty and itchy. Biting ants trooping from the nest Dzifa had disturbed made the wait even more uncomfortable. Leslie complained about needing to use the bathroom. He refused Ato's suggestion that he go behind a bush.

"Just get my phone back so we can home," Leslie moaned, crossing his legs.

"Hey!"

They spun around.

A sweaty-faced man with a face like oily chocolate and a stomach that curved over his belt was lumbering toward them. A second, even larger man charged behind him. They were surprisingly swift. Before Ato could take two steps he was in a gorilla grip.

"Look at these lizards. How did they get out?" one captor grunted.

Ato's writhing and fighting only served to tighten the grasp on him. He was hauled like a sack of potatoes around to the front where the security post was, and chucked through the black gates. He landed hard on the pitted concrete that made up the front yard of Agora. The gate closed with a sickening thud.

CHAPTER TWENTY-THREE

◊ ◊ ◊ ◊ ◊ ◊ ◊ ◊ ◊

ATO JUMPED UP, FRIGHTENED AND BEWILDERED. THE MEN were nowhere to be seen. Leslie crouched on his knees beside him, crying. Ato looked around wildly.

"Leslie, where's Dzifa?" His voice was unsteady.

Leslie remained stock-still, mute in shock. He looked as if he had been dumped on a strange planet by a UFO. A number of kids ranging in age from ten to fifteen leaned on metal railings along the open verandas of the U-shaped building, looking at them curiously. More children idled about in the open doorways and windows, chatting.

"They've taken Dzifa. To sell her," Leslie squeaked tearfully.

"Who would want to sell her?" But Ato found his voice sounded hollow. "Come on." He yanked Leslie to his feet. "Let's get Dzifa and get out of here."

He ran over to the gate and pounded on it.

"My phone's still here," Leslie whimpered.

Ato groaned. That dratted phone. "Leslie, we have to find Dzifa!"

"I know," Leslie sobbed. "You find her. I'll . . . I'll look for my phone . . . and I'll meet you—"

"No! I can't lose you too. We stay together." Ato clamped his teeth together to stop his jaw from chattering with the panic he felt. "Those boys will be easy to find. Let's get your phone back fast. Then we get Dzifa." Dear God, please let Dzifa be okay, he thought, forcing himself to calm down. Maybe she'd been locked up after biting someone.

He ran with Leslie over to a group of five boys sitting on a large stone beside a rusty water tank.

"Help us, please! Some guys threw us in here. And they took our friend. We have to find her. But we have to get our phone back first! We gave the phone to someone—a boy. Here!" Ato's words tumbled out in a frantic stream.

"You gif your phone to a boy here. His name is called what?" a boy with a ragged T-shirt asked.

"I don't know."

"You gif somebody your phone?" another boy with torn shorts asked Ato. "And you donno his name? What do he look like?"

Ato realized "two eyes" would not do as a description. He shrugged dejectedly.

The first boy made a face. "You be kwasia? Over here people steal even our underwear when we take a bath."

Leslie sniffled. "I want to go to the bathroom."

The second boy pointed to a shack with a tiny window, a few feet away. "There. But the taps are dry. No water. For three days."

Leslie ran off and disappeared inside the shack. He shot back out at once, as if he'd been chased out by a crocodile.

"I'm gonna hold it," he whispered to Ato.

A rush of fear tore through Ato. Where was Dzifa? He turned to the boys desperately. "Look—if you get us back the phone, we'll give you money. I have to find my friend!"

Leslie wrung his hands.

The eyes of the boy with the ragged T-shirt lit up greedily. "How much will you give me?"

"Ten cedis," Ato said quickly. All he wanted now was to get Dzifa. Fast. And leave.

"Gimme the money."

Leslie stifled a sob and handed over the note. "I only have ten cedis left now."

"Rich boy—you don' wanna share yo money?" Ragged T-Shirt took the money in his filthy hands, admired its crispness and stuffed it deep into his shorts. "Wait here," he said. He beckoned to the second boy and they scuttled off together.

"So why you come here to take pictures?" one of the three boys left asked Ato.

"We heard about this place from the Prophet," Ato said, his eyes roving the compound for a glimpse of Dzifa. "We heard he was doing good things."

"You wanna know things, you ask us. Don' take pictures. Nuthin' gowin' on here. We waitin' for sumtin' to happen."

His companions nodded. Ato observed the scores of children lazing around, the building with missing roof tiles, broken windows and doors, the weedy compound. It was easy to believe these boys.

"After the Prophet first bring us here, we never see him again," one boy said, scratching his dusty feet. "We were beggin' on the streets. He say he wanna help us become sumtin'—carpenter, mechanic, plumber, tailor, cook. He tell us we gonna grow up and build our own house and buy cars. So we happy and we come. But . . . plenty time pass, and we jus' here eatin' bad rice and beans and waitin'."

Same story from these boys too, Ato thought, feeling dazed. Prophet Yakayaka had asked for money to look after children. But the money was not coming here. He gave Leslie a did-you-hear-that? glance. Leslie's eyes were wide and unseeing. He seemed to be in a trance.

"Where are your parents?" he asked the boys, his eyes still roving the compound for Dzifa.

The two boys shrugged.

"My mom married some wicked guy who beat me every day," the boy with dusty feet offered. "He—"

"Hey you!"

Ato spun around.

The two boys had reappeared, with Two Eyes and Third Eye.

"You tell them that I steal your phone?" Two Eyes said to Ato accusingly.

"No, no! I didn't!"

Two Eyes shoved the boy with the ragged T-shirt. "You see! I was taking pictures for him. I no be criminal!" He handed Ato the phone. "I go back to de hole but you were not there. You wanna look at the pictures I take?"

Ato took the phone eagerly. Then a sound behind them made him turn around. The gates were sliding open. Dzifa was running in. Behind her was the taxi driver. The two large wardens who had nabbed them earlier puffed along behind them.

"There!" Dzifa pointed at Ato and Leslie.

Hot, sweet relief washed over Ato. He shoved the phone in his pocket and raced to her with Leslie on his heels.

"Dzifa!" he yelled. His throat ached from the anxiety of the last few minutes.

"You stupid children!" the taxi driver exclaimed. "Where have you been? I've been looking for you! Wait till we get home. You will be so sorry!"

The bigger warden wiped the sweat from his brow with a fat hand. "You have to control your children. Letting them run around the place like wild animals."

"God cursed me with unruly and disrespectful children," the taxi driver said. He pointed to Leslie. "This one is like his mother, my good wife. Stingy, but doesn't like trouble. As for this one with his head like a coconut"—he jabbed Ato's shoulder—"he's always running away from school. And this one—" The driver tugged on Dzifa's ear.

"Hey!" she squealed. "Watch it!"

"What!" the wardens exclaimed in unison.

"Did you just shout 'hey'? To your father?" one warden growled. His chin jutted forward, covered in untidy black hair.

"Here he is working to feed you and you repay him by running around like goats. Apologize, all of you! Properly!"

"I'm sorry, sir," Leslie wept.

"I'm sorry, sir," Ato muttered.

Dzifa grunted mutinously.

"Open your mouth!" the second warden barked.

"I'm sorry." She gave the warden a dirty look.

"Eh? Sorry what? Sorry, 'tree'? Sorry, 'grass'? Say 'I'm sorry, Daddy'!"

"I'm sorry . . . D-d-daddy."

"The girl is the worst of the lot," the taxi driver said cheerfully. "A tongue like a snake. All lip and no brain. Dim as a mushroom—always bottom of her class."

Ato noticed Dzifa bite her lower lip so hard the blood drained from it.

"You should punish them more often," the second warden offered. "We don't punish kids enough these days. Then they grow rough—like weeds."

"I would punish the girl every morning if I had my way. My wife won't hear of it."

Poking and shoving them with great relish, the taxi driver herded them out to his taxi.

It turned out that after evading the wardens, Dzifa had run to beg the taxi driver to help get Ato and Leslie out. After giving her a lecture on Why It Paid to Be Polite to Everyone Because One Never Knew, the taxi driver had agreed to pretend to the wardens that he was their father. Once they were all in the security of the dusty backseat of the taxi, the driver turned around and rebuked them colorfully and bad-temperedly. When he had run out of words, he switched on his engine, turned up his radio loud and started off on the return journey.

Ato exhaled. "Guys," he whispered, "Agoro is a crazy mess. All that food and money Prophet Yakayaka's getting at the House of Fire for the kids—he's not giving them any of it!"

"So what is he doing with that money?" Dzifa wondered aloud.

"We've got to find out. But secretly," Ato warned, looking pointedly at Leslie. "We can't tell our parents anything yet; we can't tell them where we've been today."

Leslie was not looking at Ato. He was biting his nails and tapping at his phone. "Twenty-seven messages from Mum," he moaned. Then, with a dying red blink from his battery indicator, his phone screen went black.

The taxi driver grunted tunelessly to hiplife music. Dzifa scowled at him. Ato sat staring out the car window, but he and his thoughts were hundreds of feet up in the air. So many strange and horrid surprises had popped up in the last few weeks: the dead and dying plants and animals around Turo. Choco. The suspicious drawing in the Prophet's office. The burning up of their project to Nnoma. The miserable, run-down place Agoro had turned out to be. And the dots all connected to form one picture—Prophet Yakayaka. One thing was for certain: Prophet Yakayaka was not the good man everyone in town thought he was. The Prophet had lied—to these poor kids about the care he would give them, and to the people he was taking money from for the children. He must have lied about the evil around Turo. There was no evil. There was only Prophet Yakayaka.

Ato felt his jaw tighten. His mother had warned him—*do not cross the line*. The same way Nana had warned his father about crossing the stream. But he had to expose Prophet Yakayaka. Ato was a falcon, a hunter—and the Prophet was his prey.

CHAPTER TWENTY-FOUR

◊ ◊ ◊ ◊ ◊ ◊ ◊ ◊ ◊

THERE WERE A HANDFUL OF MEMORIES ATO WISHED HE could erase from his mind forever. Choco dying was one of them. Arriving back home from Agoro was another.

To start with, the ride back from Agoro took two nail-biting, heart-thumping hours in crawling evening traffic. By the time they arrived home, it was past 7:30 p.m. and their parents and neighbors were out combing the neighborhood for them. Two men had dived into the pond, searching the bed for them.

His mother had never been so angry. "You were never like this before you went to Nana's!" she wept. "She said she would give me money to help pay my shop rent. She knew I needed it. And then she asked if she could have you every weekend. How could I say no? But the Prophet was right about her: she was pretending to help me. In fact, she was buying your soul and encouraging you to behave badly!" Then she collapsed on the couch and buried her face in her hands.

He had finished off a cold bowl of groundnut soup, then crept to his room and sat on his bed to reflect on his fate. So Nana had given Mum money in exchange for time with him? Nana must have wanted him really badly. But what for? Because she enjoyed being with him? Why couldn't she just have come to visit more often? Was there some other reason she wanted him in her home? And what did it mean to "buy" a soul?

After several minutes, a thought interrupted his fruitless musing: he hadn't seen the pictures on Leslie's phone.

You wanna look at the pictures I take? Two Eyes had asked him.

Yes he did, Ato thought. Had Two Eyes taken good pictures? Pictures that would prove that the Prophet was not the loving and kind man he pretended to be? That he wasn't giving those needy children what he had promised them? That he was a liar and a cheat?

The next day was Thursday, and it started off with an icy greeting from his mother.

"Here we were thinking Dzifa was a bad influence—all along it was you, Ato. Leslie's mother called me: Leslie is not talking. He can't say a word about yesterday. He's been robbed of his speech. He threw up his dinner. It's all because of you, Ato!"

"What did I do?"

"You forced him to take out his savings and took him on a joy ride. Now he's traumatized! His mother has taken away his phone so no one can reach him. Where did you really go?"

"We . . . we were driving around looking for a spot for a new project." His words sounded unconvincing even to his own ears.

"You're grounded for one month. After school you come home

and you stay home! I'll lock you in if I have to." Her eyes were puffy, as if she'd spent the night awake or crying.

On the way to school her phone rang. It was Dzifa's mother. Was Ato's mother really sending him off to school that day? Was that a good idea? She was keeping Dzifa in bed with a cup of hibiscus tea, she said. Dzifa needed a day to calm her nerves.

Life was so unfair, Ato thought morosely.

"Don't bother to pack your things for Nana's tomorrow." His mother's fingers tapped hard on her wheel. "I'm going to find a way to get Nana her money back. I won't let her buy your soul to destroy it. You're never going back there again."

Ato's heart sank. Please, God, he thought, Nnoma is gone. Please don't stop me from going to Nana's, too.

At school, Leslie seemed to be avoiding him. Ato finally spotted his hunched frame entering the library. He waited a few cautious minutes. When the librarian's attention was turned to a student asking intelligent questions, he sidled into the seat beside Leslie.

Leslie had a book open before him. He greeted Ato with a look of wounded agony.

"Look, Leslie, I'm sorry. I'm sorry we all got into such trouble. I know I said the trip was only going to be two hours."

Silence.

"Did you have a look at the pictures on your phone?"

Leslie flung his book aside. It landed facedown on the tiled floor. He snatched his bag and dashed out without a word. Ato looked after him, shocked. It was not like Leslie to disrespect a library book.

Leslie was not just avoiding him, Ato realized; he wouldn't even look him in the eye during the rest of their classes. Perhaps he was pretending to be traumatized. Perhaps his mother had warned him: "Never speak to Ato ever again! He's a bad boy who will lead you to a life of crime."

He needed to talk to someone badly, and he missed Dzifa. Agoro was clearly just a front. None of the money and the food and gifts the Prophet was receiving was getting to the children. Fund-raising by Agoro. He was using Agoro to raise money— a lot of it. But what was he using the money for?

Ato scratched his chin. Philomena was involved in the nasty business around Turo. He had to find out what she had done, and why she had done it. He knew the Prophet was behind it. Hopefully, armed with what Philomena would tell him, what they'd heard at Agoro, the drawing Leslie had, and any pictures on the phone, he and Dzifa could piece together what Prophet Yakayaka was up to, and expose him.

But it would have to be him and Dzifa. Leslie didn't have the spine, Ato thought, trudging to the bathroom before the last two lessons of the day. His feet felt heavy with discouragement. Would they ever get to the bottom of all this? There would be no following in his father's footsteps up to the Dawn Locus now. No Nana's. Papa Kojo was ruined. And for all those kids at Agoro—no chance that they would get the help they had been promised. It wasn't fair.

He walked through the open door of the boys' bathroom, and there was Leslie at the sink—washing his hands, scrubbing them in fact, working a thick lather between his fingers. They saw each other at the same time. Still the same wide-eyed, tormented look from Leslie.

He would try one more time, Ato thought. He needed to see those pictures. "Leslie . . ."

Leslie looked away and lathered his hands again. "I can't! I can't!"

"Look, Leslie, the pictures were the whole point of going there. All you need to do is find a way to get your phone and give it to me."

"If something happens to those kids, it will be my fault!" Leslie rinsed his hands thoroughly under the full force of the water.

Ato blinked in surprise.

Leslie was now rubbing his hands under the dryer. He finished and stumbled out, shaking his head violently. "I want to forget it. But I can't. I see it every time I shut my eyes. I keep wanting to vomit. It was so nasty. The Prophet . . . the Prophet . . . he's getting filmed again, and I'm supposed to stand beside him again this afternoon at five o'clock on TV telling people to give money to Agoro. But it's so awful there . . . I feel sick . . . I can't . . ."

A few kids walked past, casting inquisitive glances at them. Ato ignored them. He suddenly understood Leslie. "Hey"—he slipped a supportive arm around him—"were the toilets in Agoro disgusting?"

A muffled groan escaped Leslie's throat. "Ato, there was no water. When I shut my eyes, I see germs clinging to their hands, underneath their fingernails, in their eyes, their mouths. To think I told everyone on TV what a great job the Prophet was doing!"

The bathrooms must have been really bad, Ato realized. It was not fair! It was downright wicked of the Prophet to treat the children like that, and everyone had to know! Ato pressed his fists together. He wasn't going to run away from the kids at Agoro the way he had with Choco. His thoughts clicked into place.

"Leslie, if we're fast enough, then maybe this afternoon, everyone watching Sunshine TV will find out exactly what the Prophet is doing!"

"This afternoon? How? Are you mad? I can't say anything on TV! I'd be too scared! No one would believe me!" Leslie moaned.

"They will—when we show them the pictures on your phone! Leslie, get the phone, let's see what pictures the boys got. If there's anything on there, I'll show everyone. You don't need to do anything else."

"Would you? Could you?" Leslie's voice thinned to a frightened whisper. "This is Prophet Yakayaka. He's a powerful man, Ato. You can't take him down!"

"I can. I'm a falcon, Leslie. And falcons don't hunt flies."

"Huh?"

"Never mind. Let's talk about the pictures. If I could show them—"

"—then we can stop any more kids from being tricked into going there!" Leslie's lip stopped quivering. He sniffed. Then he sighed. "My mother took my phone this morning," he whispered brokenly. "She confus—conficated—"

"Confiscated it."

"Yes. For two weeks. It's in her bedside drawer. I just can't take . . . she trusts . . ." He chewed his lip hard and shifted his legs restlessly. "But I've got to help get those kids out of there. I've got to . . ." He looked distraught at the thought of what he had to do.

Ato stiffened. Would Leslie actually . . . ?

Leslie covered his face with his hands. His voice was muffled. "If the kids in Agoro get some deadly disease . . . when all the time I could have saved them just by borrowing back my phone, I'll never be able to live with myself. I'm breaking my mum's trust." He dropped his hands. "But I'll have to get . . . to take my phone back."

"Yes!" Ato grabbed Leslie's forearm. "You have to!"

The bell rang for the last lesson to begin. Slowly they made their way back to class.

Halfway to the classroom Leslie stopped. "Ato?" His tear-streaked eyes held Ato's gaze.

"What?"

"There was no rich old auntie, was there?"

Ato shook his head sheepishly. "How did you guess?"

"I wondered . . . if she was so kind, why did you need my money to get to Agoro?" He shrugged dolefully. "But I s'pose you did what you had to, Ato. Now I've got to do what I have to."

◆ ◆ ◆ ◆ ◆

And that was how that afternoon, exactly ten minutes after his mother had driven back to work, leaving Philomena with strict instructions to watch Ato, Ato was scurrying away from Leslie's house. In his pocket were both the Prophet's building drawing and Leslie's phone. He had terrified Philomena into letting him go by waving his snakeskin in her face.

On returning home, he shut his bedroom door. Switching on the phone, he tapped Gallery.

And gasped. It was worse than he'd thought.

Two Eyes had earned his money. Shot after shot after shot of pictures, cold and clear: of rooms with rotten and warped roof rafters. Broken windows. Light switches hanging loose from their sockets, with dangerous-looking electrical wires sticking out. Filthy pillows and stained mattresses on the floor. Pitted floors. Missing doors. The overgrown yard covered in clumpy weeds. Rusty poles that leaned in wearily from the weight of the shabby clothes drooping from them. Benches with missing legs in the dining hall, supported by stacks of cement blocks.

And then the bathrooms. He clapped his hands over his mouth. Black mold snaked across the discolored tiled walls. The doors to the toilets were rotten, with holes where handles should have been. The toilets themselves exceeded his grimmest expectations. He gazed at the cracked toilet basins, stained black, brown and deep yellow. Two Eyes had even photographed inside the bowl. The contents were suitably horrific. The water cistern above it contained no water, had no handle, and was moldy inside. All but one sink was broken away from the wall. The only one still attached had a crack zigzagging across it. A broken toilet bowl rested on the filthy floor. But the worst was yet to come. The video gallery revealed a storeroom with mice and roaches scurrying over sacks of rice, gari and beans. Ato exhaled grimly. Hopefully this would be enough.

Now for Philomena. It was 4 p.m. He had sixty minutes. He pressed his fists together and shut his eyes. He needed to dive, to hit his prey fast and hard. He was five thousand feet up. How could he pull this off without missing his prey, hurting himself horribly, or slamming into the ground and killing himself? Timing and force, he thought to himself. The peregrine falcon folded back his wings and tail. He tucked back his feet. The stoop had begun.

CHAPTER TWENTY-FIVE

◇ ◇ ◇ ◇ ◇ ◇ ◇ ◇ ◇

WITH SWEATING, TREMBLING FINGERS, ATO PHONED DZIFA'S mother. She answered straightaway.

No, it wasn't Leslie, he said in response to her question. It was Ato, and yes, he'd had to go to school, and yes, actually school turned out to be great. Super, in fact. He had the building drawing Dzifa had mentioned. Could he send her a picture of it from Leslie's phone? Would she please send a message back about what she thought? He ended the call, tapped the recorder button on the phone on, and slipped it into the pocket of his shorts. The solid rectangular shape of Leslie's phone felt comforting. He stepped out onto the kitchen patio.

Philomena was shaking out a tablecloth. She eyed him warily. "Bad boy. Going out when your mama said stay home. Your nana has given you strange powers, and now you think you can do anything you like."

"Why did you do it, Philo?" His voice was calm . . . with what he hoped was a thin layer of menace.

She paused at his tone, gave the sheet a brisk flap and folded it into the laundry basket.

"Answer me, Philomena."

She turned to him with a half-questioning, half-suspicious look. "Do what?"

"Why did you do it?"

"I don't know what you are talking about." She unpegged a napkin.

"You do, Philo. Turo. Why did you do it?"

The napkin slipped from her hand to the ground. Her eyes darted around, searching for invisible listeners. Something reflected in her eyes. Fear. "Wh-what are you saying, Ato?"

His heart was pounding, would she say she knew nothing?

Philomena's lips were moving noiselessly, as though the volume control in her throat was switched off. He reached into his left pocket and whipped the snakeskin out of his pocket.

"Eii!" Philomena staggered backward.

He raised the snakeskin to his ear and closed his eyes for a moment, as though listening to a silent voice. When his eyelids flickered open, his gaze was wide and staring.

"I hear you," he said aloud to an unseen speaker. "The dress she wore, black with flowers and long sleeves, and the buttons in front. The cleaning cupboard?" He spoke in a monotone, as though he were in a trance and repeating words spoken to him.

"Eii!" Philomena fell to her knees and threw up her arms.

Philomena may as well have been invisible. Ato's eyes remained unseeing as he kept the snakeskin to his ear, apparently listening to it. "She must confess," he droned flatly. "Confess what she did in Turo. If not, a snake's tongue will grow in her mouth. Black. Forked."

"Haiii! I beg you. Please." Philomena cupped her hands in a plea for her human tongue. "He . . . he said it was a bad spirit. I had to do it. Otherwise everything would die. He said, First the land! Then the animals! Then the people!"

His heart rate speeded up. It was working! "She must tell what she did there!" He struggled to keep his lips from stretching into a triumphant grin.

"Please, I beg you. I only poured the medicine. I beg you, Ato! I need my tongue. Don't make my tongue . . ." and she began to shake with wild, rasping sobs.

Still his eyes remained blank, his tone a dull chant. He needed her to tell him more, a lot more. "She must say where the medicine is."

Philo stabbed her finger toward the cleaning cupboard.

"P-p-please, it's there. Inside the cupboard."

His excitement was simmering and he struggled to maintain his appearance of a trance. "She must say where: where she poured the medicine."

Philomena wrung her hands wretchedly and wept louder.

He pressed the snakeskin against his ear again. "She must say where. If not, she will turn into a tuber of yam, in her bed, tomorrow morning."

"I beg you! He gave me the medicine for the evil spirit and I poured it in the water . . . the pond."

The pond! No wonder their project had stayed fine while everything else that used the pond water died! Summoning every ounce of willpower, he kept his gaze glassy, his tone dull and robotic. "She must say when."

"He said every Sunday night because the evil comes on Sundays!"

So that's why she was always drowsy on Mondays! He pressed on relentlessly. "She must confess what she did to the project."

"He said I should burn it. He said the evil would kill you, Ato. He said if I burned it I would save you! Please don't let it turn me into yam!" She beat her chest, tears coursing down her face.

Ato was not done with her. "She must confess who it was. Who gave her the medicine? Who made her pour it in the pond? Who made her burn the project? The name. She must mention the name!"

Philomena buried her face in her hands.

"She must say the name." He raised the snakeskin.

"Oh, Ato, why do you treat me this way? I am my mother's only daughter! Who will look after her if I turn into a tuber of yam?"

It would soon be 5 p.m. He had other arrangements to make. He lowered his hand, still clutching the snakeskin. Giving a convincing shudder, he blinked rapidly, as though he were coming around. "What are you doing on the ground, Philomena?" he asked in normal tones.

She stared at him.

He blinked once more and rushed indoors. In his bedroom, he

took out the phone and tapped the recorder button off. There was one message from Dzifa's mother.

Ato read the message. It was only a few lines, but he was numb with disbelief after he was done. How callous could a person be? There was no time to wonder. Quickly scrolling through the contact list, he found the name he was looking for and hit the call button.

A familiar voice answered. Ato spoke rapidly, stumbling over his words in his haste and nervousness.

"So I'm going to send you a picture of the drawing we have, the message from Dzifa's mum about it, the pictures from Agoro, and what I recorded from Philomena now," Ato finished. "Call me when you've got them. I want to know if that will be enough."

He ended the call and, with several taps, sent everything he had said he would. The seconds ticked by. He waited one minute. Two minutes. Five minutes. He kept glancing at the phone. The screen remained black. It was now almost 4:30 p.m. Thirty minutes to go.

He fiddled with the phone and tapped Settings . . . and groaned. All incoming calls had been blocked. He tapped Redial. The phone was answered on the first ring.

"Kid, this afternoon could finally be worth my time. Relevant news! If we got the Philomena woman to name him, that would be the clincher. Still, I say we can fly with this. Meet me by the pond. 4:45 p.m. sharp."

Yes!

By now his hands were sweaty and shaky. He tapped Dzifa's mother's number. She answered immediately.

"Thank you so, so much for explaining the drawing!" he exclaimed. "We're going to try and stop the Prophet! Can you please get Dzifa to come over to Turo? Immediately? No, we're not breaking into any buildings," he promised.

There was one last thing to do. He hurried back out to the kitchen patio, where Philomena cut a woeful picture, kneeling in her tearful state.

"Philomena, I'm sorry, but you have to mention the name." The snakeskin dangled from his hand. His expression was one of regret that the following day would find her transformed into a tuber of yam in her bed.

She shuddered violently and burst into fresh tears. "Ato, after everything I have done for you! Your washing. Ironing. Cleaning your room. And now, you want me to die?"

Ato felt a twinge of pity for her. That surprised him. After all, she had burned his project and ruined his chance of going to Nnoma. Now he was going to have to wait until another invitation opened again, and who knew when that would be? He was not supposed to feel sorry for her.

"The name, Philomena. The name."

Her shoulders slumped. "If I mention this person's name, the evil spirit in the ground will kill my mother. Then it will kill me too."

Rage flooded through him. How had she become so scared, so helpless?

"It's a lie, Philomena! It cannot kill you. It will not kill your mother. This person has made you scared because that's the only way they can get you to do their dirty work!" He paused, suddenly overwhelmed by the irony of his own words.

"Some people . . . swing a rope in your face. And you think it's a cobra so you . . ."

". . . run."

"Exactly. In the direction they want you to."

Fear couldn't be the only way—and it would make him as bad as the Prophet. He did not want that. He wanted to be like his dad.

I never felt afraid when he was with me, Yusuf had said of his dad.

There was another way. But there was very little time. Would it be enough? And would his plan work? He could only try.

He held up the snakeskin again.

CHAPTER TWENTY-SIX

◊ ◊ ◊ ◊ ◊ ◊ ◊ ◊ ◊

THE PEREGRINE FALCON'S WINGS, FOLDED BACK, GAVE HIS
body the shape of a boomerang. This reduced the air drag that
could slow him down. His head was turned at a slight angle—this
helped him see his prey best.

Ato observed Max, who was studying the blackened and
rotting stubs of what had been their project. Max spoke rapidly
into his recorder, jabbing his forefinger at his cameraman, Yaw,
who looked more alive than Ato had ever seen him. Yaw sprang
about, clicking his shutter madly at everything. The late afternoon
sunrays provided generous light, and his professional lens missed
nothing—a dead frog on the bank, small fish floating upside down
in the pond, the lifeless, discolored plants in and around the pond,
Papa Kojo's shriveled vegetables.

"Pity we don't have a picture of the dead dog. Dead things
get more views," Max muttered. Yaw grunted his disappointment.

Ato felt a stab of pain: Choco was now a Dead Thing. The
reporters satisfied themselves with a close shot of the mound of
dirt that covered her, with its decoration of withered flowers.

Papa Kojo and his sons and laborers gathered around. Their faces were lined with worry.

"We are afraid of this thing here. We canno' even sleep now. We hope Prophet Yakayaka can help us," Papa Kojo said brokenly, speaking into the recorder Max held to his lips.

"So you believe some underground evil power is doing this?" Max asked.

Papa Kojo and his group nodded vigorously.

By now it was 5 p.m. Over at the House of Fire, the Prophet was already positioning himself on the lowest step of the House of Fire. He wore a red suit. His supporters assembled around and behind him. Max's soundman was there too, testing the black loudspeakers set up in the parking lot.

Max snapped his fingers and pointed there. "Let's move."

In a slight curve, the falcon hurtled downward, headfirst, at 200 miles per hour. At his current speed, the hunting bird knew he could injure himself if he struck his prey full-on.

Dzifa was running up to the House of Fire as Ato arrived with the reporters and Papa Kojo's group.

"Ato!" Her eyes shimmered with curiosity, and she spoke in a low, excited tone. "My mother checked out the picture you sent her. She told me that in the drawing, the House of Fire is three times bigger than it is now! She said it's built completely over Papa Kojo's vegetable farm! That's why we didn't see the farm. Prophet Yak plans to build over Papa Kojo's farm! And turn our Turo into a parking lot!"

Ato gripped her hand. "I know, I read it and sent it to Max!"

"Full speed ahead now," Max said.

The falcon was a gray blur against the blue sky. His prey had not spotted him yet. The falcon's clawed feet curled into a clenched fist . . .

Ato tucked himself discreetly behind a group of broad-backed women and brought Dzifa up to speed. His mother stood smiling on the second step of the House of Fire, beside Leslie's mother. She believed her son to be at home, grounded and repentant. On the Prophet's right, Leslie stood rigidly. He looked as though his front teeth were clamped on a dead roach.

Ato scanned the crowd. Philomena was not in sight. He had left her in a crumpled heap on the kitchen patio, hoping she would follow him. Max had the full recording of her confession on Leslie's phone. But would that be enough?

"Get everyone in," Max murmured to Yaw. "Viewers need to see the crowd reaction." Yaw swung his lens around. He dipped and darted about as if he had springs in his knees.

Aside, Max whispered to Ato and Dzifa, "Viewers are gonna hear your story . . . soon. For now, stay hidden, and"—he touched his finger to his lips—"when it's your turn to talk, I'll signal. Keep it short. Keep it true. And don't be scared."

"Max. You're late." Prophet Yakayaka smiled humorlessly as the reporter approached him.

"I do apologize, Prophet Yakayaka, it was for a good cause. You are the star of our show today!" Max's voice boomed over the loudspeakers. He turned to the crowd and raised an arm in greeting. "Welcome, viewers! I'm Maximilian Odum reporting for Sunshine

TV. We're live again at the House of Fire for Giving Thursday, where for several weeks now Prophet Yakayaka has received generous donations for Agoro, his refuge for street children!"

The crowd, minus Leslie, burst into applause.

Prophet Yakayaka spread out his arms expansively. "Thank you to all our kind givers!"

Max spoke again. "Before the giving begins, perhaps the good Prophet can help answer some questions. Down by the pond a hundred yards from here, plants and animals are dying. The vegetable farm is failing for the first time in its history. Viewers at home can see pictures of this on their screens," he said. "Prophet Yakayaka, according to locals, you say this disturbing development is because of an evil presence."

A perceptible shudder swept through the people gathered.

Prophet Yakayaka's smile shifted a tad. "This is not why we are here today, Max. Yes, there is an evil presence in that area. Yes, it will be dealt with. But back to today's—"

"In fact, Prophet Yakayaka, what would you say if I suggested that the misery in that area is not due to evil, but in fact—a poison!"

The crowd gasped. Papa Kojo exclaimed aloud.

The Prophet's eyes narrowed. He gave Max a pitying look. "What do you know of evil, young man? If you knew what I have seen—"

"What would you say, Prophet Yakayaka, if I suggested that the reason for this poisonous destruction—is because you want to drive the people off the land?"

The prey had realized what was happening. It picked up speed, flying in an erratic zigzag pattern trying to evade its predator. But the falcon had anticipated this. He knew where his prey would be at the point of impact.

The Prophet's expression turned to one of thunder. "Are you mad?! Why would I drive people off? I am a man of love!"

Behind him, his supporters looked aghast, murmuring in appalled whispers at Max's shocking behavior.

Max's voice was controlled and determined. "Viewers will hear a recording now. This is the voice of a young local woman confessing that she was given a poison to pour into the local pond!"

Philomena's terrified voice played over the loudspeaker in the confession Ato had recorded on Leslie's phone. Recognizing both voices on the recording, Ato's mother gave a horrified yelp and sat abruptly on the step.

The Prophet's expression was thunderous. "You scoundrel! I don't know who that woman is or who she is talking about! Who is paying you for this?"

Max's voice spoke commandingly. "Prophet Yakayaka—your House of Fire has growing members. This building is too small. You have plans for a bigger building, one that will seat hundreds of people. People are donating generous sums to you. They believe these gifts of money and goods are for Agoro. In fact, you plan to use this money to build a massive structure on land that you intend to take from a poor vegetable farmer whom you are scaring off with stories of an evil presence!"

Papa Kojo's jaw dropped open. He spluttered incoherently. There were gasps, and protests from the gathered people.

At this point, Leslie spotted Ato and Dzifa. He melted away from the Prophet's side and reappeared beside his friends.

"You have no proof, you lying cockroach!" Prophet Yakayaka snarled.

Impact was in one millisecond. The falcon unfurled his wings. The air drag acted as brakes to avoid a deadly full-body collision. He unclenched his feet. Timing and force.

Max raised his hand. He held the map. "I do. In this drawing provided by three young investigators."

"Stolen from me!"

"So you admit this is yours!"

Three men in the Prophet's group of supporters advanced threateningly toward Max and Yaw. Papa Kojo and his sons, muscles rippling and faces heavy with menace, stepped up to block them. The Prophet's men retreated.

"Viewers at home will see on their screens a professional drawing for a new House of Fire. In this drawing the building covers the entire area beside the pond, where local farmer Papa Kojo here grows his vegetables. A bridge over the pond links the building to a large parking lot, which the Prophet plans to build over a green nature spot where children play and learn."

Another tremor of disbelief rippled through the crowd.

"This is not the job I am paying you for," Prophet Yakayaka spluttered. "Today is Giving Thursday!"

"I am paid to tell people what is really going on! Prophet Yakayaka, how much money have you raised so far for your children's refuge, Agoro? How much of that money actually went to Agoro? And would you give your permission for us to conduct a live interview at Agoro?"

"All the money raised has gone to helping those children!"

Max faced Yaw's recorder lens, his voice loud and clear over the loudspeakers. "Viewers will now see footage of Agoro on their screens, and candid pictures of the deplorable conditions under which the neglected children of Agoro live."

"What nonsense is this?" Prophet Yakayaka barked. His face was tight with rage. The people around leaned in closer, drinking in every word.

"This footage was captured through the action of three young local investigators! They will now tell their story." He signaled to Ato and Dzifa, who sidled out from the cover of the large women. Leslie shuffled out to stand beside them.

The falcon's talons, now fully extended, ripped into his prey. A cloud of feathers erupted from the prey. A red spray spouted out.

"Ato! Leslie!" their mothers shrieked in unison.

"You!" Prophet Yakayaka roared. He lunged at the children. But a thick, calloused hand grabbed him by one shoulder, bringing him to a snapping halt. Papa Kojo held him in a bear grip. His sons and laborers formed a solid wall around him. Papa Kojo's middle son took the drawing from Max. He held it close to his face, tracing a finger over it. His brother peered over his shoulder at it. He scowled, turned to the Prophet and raised his fist ominously.

Max plunged ahead. "Viewers now see Ato Turkson, the leader, and his friends, Dzifa Mensah and Leslie Quaye. Ato Turkson leaked a disturbing story to Sunshine TV about the poisoning of a fertile stretch of land that supports vegetable production in this community. Ato and his friends had one desire: to be selected for entry to the exclusive bird reserve Nnoma, which Ato's late father helped to build. Their hope of entering Nnoma was cruelly crushed when their organic vegetable project was burned. Undeterred, they launched an investigation. They found this map in the Prophet's office. They visited Agoro and found neglected children living in unsanitary conditions! Poor food. No lessons. Terrible toilets."

Leslie groaned and cupped both hands over his mouth. Yaw zoomed his lens toward him.

"As you can see, the very memory is distressing for this particularly delicate young man," Max declared.

"Lies!" the Prophet croaked.

"The leader of the three, Ato Turkson, who obtained the confession from the local woman, will now share what he knows."

"Shut your son up!" the Prophet shrieked at Ato's mother.

Ato's heart fluttered like a trapped creature in his throat. His mother's gaze slid from him to the Prophet and back to him. He could read in her eyes her dismay and distress. She was probably sorry he was her son. She probably wished he'd never been born. Maybe she even wished him dead.

"Speak, Ato." His mother's voice was tremulous but clear.

Ato looked at her in disbelief.

She turned to the Prophet and raised both hands as if to say, Enough. Then she nodded to Ato. "Speak, my son."

Stunned and mortally wounded, the prey tumbled toward the ground. The falcon wheeled around and dived after it.

Ato spoke. With Max's microphone to his lips, the story tumbled out, relayed over the loudspeaker. He answered Max's questions, starting with their dream of Nnoma. Leslie wept as he told about their visit to Agoro. Dzifa chipped in their rescue by the taxi driver. The crowd was getting a better show than they'd expected. They drank in every word.

Ato's mother did not take her eyes off him, shaking her head and mumbling to herself, as if she was waking up from a trance. Drawn by news of exciting goings-on at the House of Fire, a larger crowd had gathered. Yaw zipped about like a cricket, recording from all angles, capturing every expression of horror, every gasp from the crowd.

Dzifa elbowed Ato and pointed. A figure was half running, half stumbling up the red dirt lane toward them.

Ato seized Max's arm. "That's Philo!"

Ato sped the short distance to her, and took her hand. It was cold, shaky and clammy. Her eyes flickered with uncertainty . . . and something else. Anger. Yaw filmed them closely as the two approached the front steps of the House of Fire.

Philomena pointed an unsteady hand at the Prophet.

Hemmed in by Papa Kojo and his band of men, the Prophet could only glower at her. Philomena gurgled, as if her words were rolling back down her throat. Max's microphone hovered below her trembling lips.

Ato squeezed her hand. "Philo," he whispered urgently, "remember how I tore the snakeskin up. And spat on it. It has no power over you. And he has no power over you either!"

"Philomena, ignore their lies! Ignore their mischief!" the Prophet shouted.

Philomena's arm steadied. She withdrew her hand from Ato. She took a step forward. Then she spat on the ground.

Ato clenched his fists and punched the air.

Philomena's hand still pointed at the Prophet. "Prophet Yakayaka—you said it was medicine for the evil spirits. You said if I did not pour the poison in the water, everyone would die. You said if I did not burn the children's project, the evil would kill everyone. You said I would die if I told anyone. You."

"She is mad!" Prophet Yakayaka howled to the stupefied crowd.

"I am not mad." Her eyes glistened with unshed tears. "I am afraid, but I am not mad." She wiped away a tear. Ato squeezed her hand proudly.

Yaw's lens zoomed in on the Prophet, who swung a fist at him. Clearly used to filming bad-tempered people, Yaw ducked like a squirrel. Prophet Yakayaka lost his balance and toppled to the ground.

The prey had hit the ground hard. The falcon landed on it with his full body weight, pinning it down. The crippled prey fluttered frantically, desperately. The falcon slashed twice: Once with his deadly hooked beak across his prey's neck. The second was with its claw across the prey's belly. A fountain of blood erupted. A pool of blood formed around the prey. Then it lay still.

Papa Kojo hauled the Prophet up by the lapels of his red suit. His shiny shoes dangled inches above the ground.

"My vegetables. My land. My time, my money!" Papa Kojo's usual smile had vanished. In its place was a murderous look. He closed his hand around the Prophet's neck. His three sons had circled around him, muscles flexing. Their expressions were equally unpleasant. Prophet Yakayaka looked around wildly.

"We were going to Nnoma. You destroyed our project! And you cheated the children!" Ato exclaimed bitterly.

"And you killed Choco!" Dzifa yelled.

"Dysentery. Typhoid . . . poor kids," Leslie rasped.

"You would have poisoned us next!" someone shouted.

"You traumatized my son!" Leslie's mother swung her yellow handbag at him. Luckily for the Prophet, she had a poor aim, and her bag bounced harmlessly off Papa Kojo's brawny back. "You wicked man!" she wailed.

Prophet Yakayaka was cowering. His supporters' expressions had shifted from adoration to uncertainty.

Max was speaking rapidly, "Maximilian Odum reporting live for Sunshine TV. Breaking news—Prophet Yakayaka of the House of Fire may need police protection as angry locals turn on him demanding answers . . ."

He paused and pressed his hand to his earpiece, listening.

His eyes registered surprise. Then he spoke again into his microphone. "News coming in from the station. Nnoma is on the line to Sunshine TV. I repeat, Nnoma is on the line. They're asking to speak to the three children. They're asking to speak to the defenders of the land, Asafo." He handed an earpiece to Ato.

Stunned, Ato placed it to his ear.

CHAPTER TWENTY-SEVEN

◊ ◊ ◊ ◊ ◊ ◊ ◊ ◊ ◊

"DIABOLICAL." ATO'S MOTHER SET DOWN HER GLASS, frothing with a green liquid. She shook her head.

"And here I was thinking dandelion, mint and pineapple was one of my better smoothies," Nana said with a smile.

Ato's mother laughed. "No, this is delicious, Nana. I meant Prophet Yakayaka; I can't wrap my head around it. I trusted him so deeply."

Ato placed his hand over his mother's. It rested on her lap, still. He slipped his other hand through Nana's. She squeezed his hand. He was sitting between his mother and Nana on a spacious new sofa. It was covered in soft green fabric and had a rounded base on which they rocked gently. He had arrived at Nana's after school that afternoon with Mum, to find that the old sofa had been removed from the porch. It stood at the bottom of the steps. Nana had not answered when he'd asked her why it was there.

"I've been afraid for so long," his mother said. Her hand curled around Ato's. "When the Prophet first arrived, five years ago, I told him that I was afraid I was doing a bad job with you, Ato. I told him how helpful Nana had been. Then"—her gaze lowered—"the Prophet told me everything that could go possibly wrong with you. He made me more afraid."

She turned to Nana. "He told me history repeated itself, that Ato might die on the sofa the way his father had died. I became afraid of you, Nana. Afraid of your home, the sofa. I thought he was helping me keep Ato safe. I felt grateful that he was saving me and Ato with his advice and warnings. He said he wanted to help many more people, he needed money for that. So, over time, I gave him all the money I'd saved up over years."

Regret crept into her voice. "I was so blind. Since yesterday, many people in our community now realize Prophet Yakayaka wasn't what he pretended to be. We thought he was a caring person. But all along he just stoked our secret fears. We became more afraid, but we all gave him more money, because we felt thankful for what he was 'saving' us from, and we wanted him to save other people too."

Her lip twisted. "To think he was planning to scare off Papa Kojo, buy his land cheaply and use our money to build a magnificent new House of Fire over it!"

Nana's hoop earrings swung as she shook her head in disgust. "The Prophet had become bolder, more ambitious. It was all about his personal greed and power. None of it was about helping people. And that's sad, because there are genuine leaders out there, who are honest about loving and helping people, and folk are going to mistrust some of them now."

Ato had heard on the news that Social Services had closed

down Agoro. All the children had been resettled in better places. The House of Fire was now silent. And the Prophet was under investigation by the police.

"I gave so much money to the Prophet," his mother admitted. "Eventually I didn't have enough to pay bills at the shop. Without asking, Nana sensed I had no money. She stepped in, and gave me a large sum of money to help out."

"But I wanted something back," Nana said, stroking her dangling earrings. "I wanted to drive away that fear. Every time I came to visit, I could sense fear taking over you, seeping into Ato. When my son was a boy, I too lived in fear that I'd make mistakes, and he'd grow up wrong. I didn't want that fear for either of you. The Prophet was clever; he recognized I might block you from him. And he didn't want that. So he fed your fears about me."

"And I got something back too!" His mother's face glowed. "I realized what a brave and smart son I had. I'd never seen that. All I saw was mischief. Now look—my brave son and his friends are among the first this year to be selected for Nnoma. Ato, you're actually going to Nnoma!" The joy in his mother's voice brought a grin to Ato's face. She hugged him. "Your father would have been so proud of you, Ato. I am so proud of you. And I'm sorry I didn't believe in you enough."

Nana's eyes shone with satisfaction.

"For me, the best part of yesterday was when Philo pointed at the Prophet and confronted him. I prayed hard, but I didn't know whether she would be able to do it," Ato said to them.

"Tell Nana again how you got Philo to be brave enough to speak," his mother chuckled. He hadn't seen her look so light-hearted in a long time.

Nana laughed aloud when he told her how he had at first terrified Philomena with the snakeskin. "That was wicked of you, Ato! Just the thing your father would probably have done!"

Ato gave a cheeky grin. "It worked. She stayed out of my closet." His face sobered. "It got her to spill out what she'd done to the pond—creeping there at midnight and pouring in poison."

"I'd noticed a change—she always looked so tired on Mondays and her work got sloppy," his mother said. "Now I understand why."

"And then when I was trying to make her confess the Prophet's name, I was going to use the snakeskin again. I saw how scared she was—of me, of the Prophet. And then I remembered what you said about fear, Nana—how people used it to get others to do what they wanted. And I didn't want to be that kind of person. I didn't want to be like the Prophet. So I took out the snakeskin again, and I held it up. She was crying and saying she didn't want to turn into a tuber of yam. And I ripped it to pieces. She was shocked. I told her it was just an old useless snakeskin that had no power. And I spat on the shreds on the floor. And told her she could spit too. And if nothing happened to her after she did, she would know the Prophet's spirits wouldn't harm her either. And I left it on the floor there with her and ran to meet Max at Turo."

His mother smiled proudly. "And she told me that after you left, she spat on it too! You helped her do the brave thing."

"You've brought up a fine, courageous boy, Mina," Nana said.

"I should say that to you, Nana. The Prophet kept warning me about your spirit. But now I know what spirit you have. The Spirit of Courage. You breathed it into Ato, and you've done more to make him brave than I have."

"I wasn't always like this." Nana's tone was wistful.

"But that's in the past, isn't it, Nana?" Ato said.

He sat between his mother and Nana in comfortable silence, sipping Nana's refreshing mint, dandelion leaf and pineapple smoothie. The sounds of Friday evening goings and comings drifted over the air. In a month's time they would be going to Nnoma! It was all he could do not to tear around Nana's garden like an electric hare. Yusuf had called on Nana's phone and had been just as thrilled. Even Leslie was excited about it: spending part of his nest egg on the trip to Agoro had ended up being a good investment after all, he'd told Ato. Dzifa had started packing.

Ato allowed himself a spontaneous grin. He would see the thousands of bird species. He would climb the Dawn Locus, see the sunrise and the falcons' roost. He would search for what his father had left on the island. Max had asked him to let him know if there was anything relevant in Nnoma. He wouldn't need to call the reporter, Ato knew. What could possibly go wrong on a famous bird paradise?

The sound of Nana's gate swinging open interrupted his reverie. Two men with arms like professional boxers stepped in and strode up to the porch steps. Their baggy tank tops could have been white—once upon a time. Each gripped a shovel. The whiff of sweat and oily skin hit Ato's nostrils.

Nana stood up, responding to their greeting. "There it is," she said, pointing to the old orange sofa below the porch. Ato and his mother exchanged perplexed glances as the workmen grabbed the sofa by its arms and lifted it as though it were a pillow. Nana walked ahead of them down the curved garden path. The workmen followed her toward the shady patch at the bottom of the garden. At the grave, Nana stopped.

"Nana, no!" Ato exclaimed, finally realizing what was going to happen. The final mystery was becoming clear.

But Nana nodded gently. "Yes, Ato."

"But . . . but . . ." A lump formed in his throat. That was where his dad was born. That was where his dad had played with his best friend. That was where his dad had died. Years later, that was where the falcon in Ato had learned to use speed, intelligence, and courage to cross the line. And that had ended up being a good thing. Like his father crossing the stream.

The workmen held the sofa above the rectangular hole. Nana nodded. "One . . . two . . ." they chanted. On "three," they let go. The sofa landed at the bottom with a dull thud. Ato's eyelids prickled.

Nana held him close and murmured above his head. "This sofa reminds me of many sad yesterdays. I need to bury them, leave them in the past and enjoy new todays. Your father is not here and I haven't been able to let go of him. I've kept this old sofa because it makes me feel I'm keeping him alive. But it's time to say goodbye to him properly. Because you are here, and that means everything to me."

His mother nodded. "I'm burying my old fears, too," she said quietly.

Ato recalled the conversations he'd overheard between his mother and the Prophet; how he'd felt he was a disappointment to his mother, and would never be as good as his father. He had to bury those thoughts in the grave too.

Nana nodded again, and the workmen dug their shovels into the soil heap beside the grave. The dark soil scattered over the orange fabric. Shovel after shovel of soil was dumped over the seats, and soon they were covered in dirt. Still the workmen continued, breathing heavily as they worked.

Ato kept his eyes on the slowly disappearing sofa. "Goodbye," he whispered.

Then he was rising into the sky on powerful wings. Far below him, dirt thudded onto the top of the backrest, covering the past, until the last glimpse of orange disappeared under the black earth. Ahead of him, through the cloud, loomed a mountain—his target, Nnoma. He was trained to reach his target every time, and he had been good enough to get there.

ACKNOWLEDGMENTS

◊ ◊ ◊ ◊ ◊ ◊ ◊ ◊ ◊ ◊

Many hands have helped me to write this book:

My agent, Sarah Odedina, who believed in me.

My editor, Helen Thomas, for pushing me to raise my game.

The Norton Young Readers team, for polishing and perfecting my work.

Mr. Osei-Afriyie and the Kwadwoan team, for giving me a platform to grow from.

My husband, Rami—always my first reader, supportive and dependable.

My children Alia, Rami B, Rima—long-suffering proofreaders, day and night.

My father, Anthony Kojo Sackey, who kept my ink flowing.

And my entire family—Sackey, Kofi, and Baitie—from whom I first learned what love is.

Thank you and God bless you.

ABOUT THE AUTHOR

◊ ◊ ◊ ◊ ◊ ◊ ◊ ◊ ◊

Elizabeth-Irene Baitie is the director of a medical laboratory. She holds an MSc in Clinical Biochemistry with Molecular Biology from the University of Surrey, UK. "Working in a lab is about running tests and making discoveries," she says. "Life is like that. You don't realize who you are until you're tested."

Her stories for children and young adults simultaneously tug at and thrill the heart. Her first children's book, *A Saint in Brown Sandals*, won the Macmillan Writer's Prize for Africa. Subsequent young adult novels—*The Twelfth Heart, The Dorm Challenge, Rattling in the Closet*, and *The Lion's Whisper*—were awarded the Burt Award for African Young Adult Literature. She has had seven novels published to date and lives in vibrant Accra with her husband. They are parents to three largely grown-up children. Her website is www.elizabethirenebaitie.com.

ABOUT ACCORD BOOKS

◇ ◇ ◇ ◇ ◇ ◇ ◇ ◇ ◇

Accord works with authors from across the African continent to provide support throughout the writing process and secure regional and international publishing and distribution for their works. We believe that stories are both life-affirming and life-enhancing, and want to see a world where all children are delighted and enriched by incredible stories written by African authors.